Coping with

DIABETES

Pat Kelly

THE ROSEN PUBLISHING GROUP, INC./NEW YORK

Published in 1998 by The Rosen Publishing Group, Inc.
29 East 21st Street, New York, NY 10010

Cover Photo by Christine Innamorato

First Edition

Library of Congress Cataloging-in-Publication Data

Kelly, Pat.
    Coping with diabetes / Pat Kelly.
        p.   cm. -- (Coping)
    Includes bibliographical references and index.
    Summary: Discusses the types and causes of diabetes, how the disease
is diagnosed and treated, and ways of managing this condition and its
impact on your life.
    ISBN 0-8239-2549-8
    1. Diabetes--Juvenile literature. 2. Diabetes in children--Juvenile liter-
ature. [1. Diseases.] I. Title. II. Series.
    RC660.5.K44   1998
    616.4'62--dc21

                                                            97-49084
                                                                CIP
                                                                AC

Manufactured in the United States of America.

About the Author

Pat Kelly works for Buistmore, Smythe, and McGee as a Software Specialist in Charleston, South Carolina. Ms. Kelly also volunteers in assisting low-income adults to improve their basic reading, writing, and math skills.

She graduated summa cum laude from the College of Charleston in 1989 with a BA in History and Political Science. She also has a joint master's degree from the University of Charleston and the University of South Carolina.

Over the years, Ms. Kelly has published writings ranging from fiction to editorials. She lives in Charleston with her husband, George, her two children, Demian and Adam, and a variety of pets.

Contents

WHAT IS DIABETES?

Diabetes Mellitus or diabetes is a metabolic disorder that results from an imbalance of hormones produced in the pancreas. People with diabetes aren't able to properly convert the food they eat into fuels needed by the body to function. This can be dangerous because without fuel, the body is unable to function properly. Not too long ago, people didn't know what diabetes was or how to treat it. In those days, people who had diabetes often died as a result of their inability to convert food into the energy needed by the body to function. We now know what diabetes is and how to treat it to help those with diabetes live normal and healthy lives. However, we still don't know what exactly causes it, and there is no cure for diabetes yet.

Diabetes affects almost 16 million people in the United States and millions more worldwide. It is not contagious. It cannot be spread from person to person. No one can catch it from you. It is called a syndrome, which is a collection of diseases. This means there is more than one type of diabetes. It is also something that often goes undiagnosed for a long time. Diabetes has a long incubation period, which is why many children are not diagnosed until puberty.

Having diabetes does not mean you will not be able to live a full and productive life. Having diabetes will not affect your goals or your dreams. There are many people

1

who have diabetes and are able to live happy and healthy lives. Actresses Halle Berry and Mary Tyler Moore, professional baseball player Ron Santos, and professional basketball player Chris Dudley are just some of the people who did not let diabetes stop them from achieving their dreams. Don't let it stop you.

The Role of the Pancreas

The pancreas, located behind the stomach, is a long, thin organ about the length of a hand. The pancreas is the organ that is responsible for the development of diabetes. The pancreas has two different types of cells, called alpha and beta cells, which produce a number of hormones. These hormones are responsible for breaking down the food that enters the body, turning it into fuel that can be used by the body, and distributing it to the various parts of the body that need the fuel.

Most of the food we eat is converted into a simple sugar called glucose. Glucose is the main energy provider for the majority of bodily functions. The glucose level in the blood fluctuates in response to a person's daily activities, from eating a meal to exercising to stressful situations. But the level always falls into set parameters.

The pancreas produces three hormones in the process of converting food into fuels usable by the body. When the level of glucose in the body rises, it signals the pancreas to produce a hormone called insulin. This usually occurs after a meal. Insulin signals muscle and fat tissue to absorb the amount of glucose it needs for daily activities. Glucose that is in the blood is called "blood sugar."

Glucose that is not needed for the body at that time is stored in the liver in the form of a starch called glycogen. The body can access this reservoir of fuel whenever the body needs it. Another hormone produced by the pancreas's alpha cells is called glucagon and is responsible for breaking down the glycogen and causing it to be released into the bloodstream for the body to use. This in effect raises the level of blood sugar.

In a person without diabetes, the amount of the two hormones produced is balanced. If, however, the glucose level increases and the body is unable to use it because the level of insulin is insufficient or the body resists the hormone, then diabetes results. Without enough insulin, cells cannot use the glucose in the blood. It also means that excess glucose cannot be stored in the liver and muscles, and when the glucose reaches a certain level, the body will force it out as waste.

What Causes Diabetes?

The body's immune system plays an important role in the development of diabetes. The immune system protects us from foreign substances that may enter our bodies, such as viruses and bacteria. For some reason that scientists have yet to understand, the immune system of people with diabetes seeks out the cells that produce insulin and destroys them. This causes people with diabetes to stop producing insulin partially or completely. Without the presence of insulin, diabetes develops. Scientists are still trying to discover what exactly causes the immune system to attack these cells.

3

Heredity plays a role in determining who will develop diabetes, especially for Type II diabetes. You are at a higher risk for developing diabetes if someone in your family has or has had diabetes.

Types of Diabetes

Diabetes is divided into two main types: insulin dependent and non-insulin dependent. They are sometimes mistakenly called "sugar diabetes."

Type I Diabetes

Insulin-dependent diabetes or Insulin Dependent Diabetes Mellitus (IDDM) is called Type I diabetes. In the past it was called juvenile-onset diabetes because it seemed to appear only during childhood or adolescence. Now doctors know that it can appear at any time in life. It is an auto-immune disorder that stems from the destruction of the insulin-producing cells in the pancreas. The body produces little or no insulin, and is unable to lower the level of glucagon. The glucagon accumulates in the blood, raising a person's blood sugar level. This is called *hyperglycemia* or high blood sugar. When the blood sugar level gets too high, glucose is removed from the body in urine as waste. Because most waste is removed from the body in urine, a person with high blood sugar may go to the bathroom as often as his or her body gets rid of the extra glucose. Frequent urination can result in a loss of water because water is a main component of urine. This may cause a person to feel very thirsty or experience a dry mouth. Dehydration can cause dry skin and blurry vision.

Also, if cells cannot get the glucose they need, they "starve." This may make a person feel very hungry even when he or she has just finished eating. If someone has diabetes, his or her body does not have the fuel it needs; that person may often feel weak and tired. Weight loss may also occur as the body's demands for fuel force the breakdown of fat cells. High glucose levels may also damage nerves which may result in a tingling feeling in the feet or leg cramps at night. High glucose levels also interfere with the action of white blood cells, which can slow the healing of cuts. High glucose levels make it easier for bacteria to grow and may result in a variety of skin infections.

If hyperglycemia is not treated, the result can be *diabetic ketoacidosis* (DKA) *coma*. When there is a lack of insulin, the body looks for alternative fuel. That alternative fuel is fat. When fat is broken down into energy, it produces a poisonous waste called ketones. Ketones will accumulate in the blood and eventually the urine. Eventually if the condition is not treated, the person will lose consciousness and possibly die.

Insulin-dependent diabetes affects males and females equally. Treatment for Type I diabetes includes daily injections of insulin to help the body use the glucose it needs. Insulin treatment is often balanced with diet and exercise.

Type II Diabetes

Type II diabetes, or Non-Insulin Dependent Diabetes Mellitus (NIDDM), usually, but not always, occurs in people who are overweight. This is also called insulin resistance. It used to be called adult-onset diabetes because it normally occurred in adults over the age of forty. But as

5

with Type I diabetes, doctors realized that Type II diabetes could appear at any time as well. Type II diabetes often strikes those who are overweight or obese.

In Type II diabetes, the body doesn't produce enough insulin, or it produces enough but the body doesn't use insulin properly or the body resists it. When Type II diabetes is diagnosed in young people, it is called Maturity Onset Diabetes in the Young or MODY. Type II diabetes affects mostly females, but it affects males as well. You are at higher risk for developing Type II diabetes if someone in your family has it and you are overweight or obese.

This type of diabetes is usually treated with a combination of diet and exercise. Some people with Type II diabetes are also treated with insulin. Weight loss will also help the body use the insulin better.

Gestational Diabetes

Gestational diabetes is another form of diabetes that occurs only in pregnant women. About 3 percent of all pregnant women develop this form of diabetes, and most of them have no prior history of any type of diabetes. (If a woman has been diagnosed with diabetes before she became pregnant, she has pregestational diabetes.) So far no one knows what causes gestational diabetes, but scientists have some ideas. Hormones from the placenta that help the baby grow also inhibit the mother's ability to absorb glucose. This causes insulin resistance. This can lead to high levels of glucose in the blood or hyperglycemia. The treatment for gestational diabetes is a combination of careful diet, exercise, and sometimes insulin injections. The American Diabetes Association (ADA) believes that all women should be tested for gestational diabetes when they are about six months pregnant, which is when insulin requirements for the mother rise. After the mother gives birth, her insulin resistance usually disappears. Women who have had gestational diabetes frequently develop it again during subsequent pregnancies. Many of them also develop Type II diabetes later in life. Diabetes II is also caused by *insulin resistance*. Proper diet and exercise are important tools in a healthy lifestyle and will help prevent or delay the onset of Type II diabetes and its many complications.

Brittle Diabetes

Brittle diabetes occurs when a person's blood sugar level goes from one extreme to the other for no apparent reason. This rising and falling cannot be predicted and may not be preceded by any symptoms. Sometimes ,people confuse brittle diabetes with Type I diabetes or refer to teenagers with diabetes as having brittle diabetes. This is because of the fluctuations in blood glucose levels that occur during puberty. This is not brittle diabetes. The blood sugar of people with brittle diabetes is frequently out of control. Brittle diabetes is also called *unstable diabetes* or *labile diabetes.*

There is another disease with the name "diabetes," *Diabetes Insipidus*. Diabetes Insipidus is NOT diabetes. It is a disease caused by a lack of a hormone produced in the pituitary gland, which is in the brain, and not the lack of insulin, which is produced in the pancreas.

7

The History of Diabetes

Diabetes has been around for a long time. It was first described in Egyptian writings in 1500 B.C. In 230 B.C., a man named Aretaeus is believed to have labeled the disease *diabetes,* which is from a Greek word meaning "to siphon." One of the symptoms of diabetes is excessive urination. The word "diabetes" was used to describe how water seemed to pass right through the body of a person with the disease. The urine of a person with diabetes contains a lot of extra sugar because the body is unable to break it down effectively. In 1679, a doctor tasted the urine of a person diagnosed with diabetes and said it was as sweet as honey and the word mellitus, which is Latin for "honey," was added to the term diabetes.

The treatment for diabetes has varied throughout the centuries, from drinking fruit wines, to taking lukewarm baths, to bloodletting, to today's use of insulin.

The History of Insulin

In 1889, Dr. Joseph von Mering and Dr. Oskar Minkowski, who believed there was a direct relationship between the pancreas and diabetes, began experimenting with dogs. They removed the pancreas from a healthy dog. The dog did not die immediately but began to urinate a lot—which is a symptom of diabetes. The sweetness of the urine puddles attracted flies. Eventually the dog went into a coma and died. The link between the pancreas and diabetes was established, and then the search began to determine what it was about the pancreas that caused diabetes.

About the same time, Paul Langerhans of Germany, a medical student, was studying the pancreas. He grew curious about some cells that looked different from most of the other cells of the organ. These cells were named the islets of Langerhans. Other scientists experimented with the islets of Langerhans and determined that, if they were removed from the pancreas, diabetes developed. In 1910, Dr. Sharpey-Shaffer of Scotland decided that a chemical he called "insulin" was missing from the pancreas of people with diabetes.

In 1921, doctors Frederick Banting and Charles Best continued the experiments of Mering and Minkowski. But they carried the experiment one step further. The scientists believed that insulin was manufactured in the pancreas in the islets of Langerhans. First they removed the pancreas from healthy dogs, causing them to develop diabetes. They then took fluid from the islets of Langerhans in healthy dogs—those which still had their pancreases—and injected it into the sick dogs. The effect on the sick dogs was dramatic. It stopped their symptoms. Shortly thereafter, Banting and Best teamed with J. B. Collip to extract a more refined insulin from cattle. The next year insulin was tried for the first time on a patient, Dr. Joe Gilchrist, with great success.

Until the 1980s, the only type of insulin available for people with diabetes came from the pancreas of animals, mostly cows and pigs. There are a variety of insulins available today: beef, pork, beef-pork combinations, and more recently human insulin. The human insulin is made from a combination of pork insulin (because pork insulin is the closest to human insulin) and genetic engineering. Human insulin is becoming the most popular of all insulin because of its purity and its fast absorption into the bloodstream.

9

Diagnosing Diabetes

Many people are unaware of the symptoms of diabetes. It's important to recognize these symptoms and seek out medical attention immediately if you experience any of these symptoms. Many people who have diabetes, especially Type II diabetes, are unaware they have the disease. Diabetes can be fatal if it is not treated properly. The sooner you find out, the sooner you can treat it.

These are the general symptoms that many people with diabetes experience:

- Frequent urination. This is called *polyuria.*

- Extreme thirst or dry mouth. This is called *polydypsia.*

- Dry skin.

- Constant hunger. This is called *polyphagia.*

- Tiredness and weakness.

- Weight loss.

- Blurry vision.

- Numbness or tingling in feet.

- Skin infections or slow-to-heal cuts.

Although not everyone who has these symptoms has diabetes, not everyone who has diabetes has all or even some of these symptoms. However, the only way to be sure is to be tested for diabetes by a doctor.

Tests for Diabetes

If you have some of these symptoms, your doctor should do a screening test. A screening test requires a drop of blood and can tell your doctor if you might have diabetes. If this test indicates diabetes is likely, the doctor will then perform a diagnostic test which will determine whether you have diabetes.

These are some of the tests your doctor might perform:

Fasting Plasma Glucose Test

For this test, you fast overnight, usually ten to sixteen hours. Then the doctor takes a sample of your blood for analysis. Normal fasting plasma glucose levels are less than 115 mg/dL. Mg/dL stands for milligrams per deciliter. A deciliter is $\frac{1}{10}$ of a liter. A milligram is $\frac{1}{1000}$ of a gram. (A paper clip weighs a gram). For every deciliter of blood, normal fasting glucose levels should show less than 110 milligrams. If the test is higher than that, the doctor will do the test again. In the past, if two or more tests show a glucose level greater than 140 mg/dL, the doctor will tell you that you have diabetes. With the new ADA guidelines, doctors consider fasting glucose levels above 110 milligrams to indicate the possibility of diabetes. A person who has a fasting glucose level of 110 to

125 mg/dL is considered to have *impaired* ability to process glucose. A person whose fasting glucose level is 126mg/dL or more is considered to have *provisional diabetes* until another test on another day confirms the same results—if that is the case, the person is considered to have diabetes.

Although the ADA has decided that the fasting glucose tolerance test is sufficient to diagnose diabetes, some doctors may recommend the Oral Glucose Tolerance Test. Ask if this test is absolutely necessary, because it can be very expensive and unpleasant.

Oral Glucose Tolerance Test
You fast overnight with this test as well. In the morning, the doctor tests a blood sample. Then you drink about 75 grams of glucose. Then your blood is tested at intervals, five times during three hours to measure your glucose levels. A person without diabetes will show a quick rise and fall in glucose levels while a person with diabetes will show a rise that will not come down very quickly. The Oral Glucose Tolerance Test does not determine whether you have diabetes, but it does indicate Impaired Glucose Tolerance. If your doctor suspects diabetes, he or she will order additional tests before a diagnosis can be made.

C-peptide test
This is another blood test done after overnight fasting. The C-peptide test is given to determine how much insulin a person produces. In a person with Type I diabetes, these peptide levels will measure zero, which indicates no

insulin. In a person with Type II diabetes, the peptide range will be normal or above normal, which indicates plenty or too much insulin.

Islet-Cell Antibody Test

Scientists have developed an antibody test that predicts if a person will eventually develop diabetes. This test is often given to those who have family members with diabetes and want to know if they will develop the disease as well. Because diabetes develops over a long period of time, researchers are able to identify people who will get the disease before it develops. The islet-cell antibody test is used to detect the presence of this particular antibody in a person's bloodstream. Not every family member feels a need to know ahead of time if he or she is going to develop a disease. If someone does wants to know, this test is available. It is important to get proper counseling before anyone gets any sort of test that predicts the future occurrence of any disease.

Diabetes and Other Health Concerns

Before the discovery of insulin, diabetes was a fatal disease. Although advances in medical science have allowed people with diabetes to live long and healthy lives, there is still no cure, and diabetics still face an increased risk for other health problems. Over a long period of time, diabetes can cause problems with your eyes, kidneys, heart, feet, skin, and nerves. This is why it is so important to know how to care for yourself properly and keep your diabetes under control. What you do now to take care of yourself can affect your future. Studies show that people who keep a tight control over their diabetes substantially reduce the risks of developing complications later on. Keeping yourself healthy will decrease your risk of developing some of these conditions, but you should still know the risks that every person with diabetes faces.

Diabetes and Your Eyes

People with diabetes need to take good care of their eyes by having regular eye exams. A common eye problem that occurs in people with diabetes is near-sightedness. This occurs when high glucose levels cause different body chemicals to accumulate in the lens of the eye. The lens swells slightly and can cause vision blurriness. This is a temporary problem that can come and go with fluctuations in blood sugar levels and does not always mean you need glasses. If you experience this and go for an eye exam, be sure to mention that you have diabetes and that your glucose levels have been going up and down. Your eye doctor, or ophthalmologist, might recommend waiting a little while until your blood sugar stabilizes before determining if you need glasses. A more serious eye disease is *diabetic retinopathy*. This occurs when the small vessels in the back of the eye break and cause damage. Diabetic retinopathy is the major contributor to blindness in the United States. Controlling your blood sugar can prevent this.

Researchers have found that keeping your blood pressure under control can also reduce the risk of diabetic retinopathy. Seventy percent of people with Type I diabetes eventually develop this complication. Because this disease can develop rapidly during puberty no matter what type of diabetes you have, it is extremely important to have REGULAR EYE CHECKUPS every year. If your blood sugar is under control, chances are your vision is very good. Blurry vision can be a symptom of hypoglycemia or hyperglycemia, not necessarily eye disease. You can have diabetic retinopathy and still have good vision. Fortunately, there are things that can be done to prevent blindness in people diagnosed with diabetic retinopathy. Laser surgery can reduce the loss of vision by up to 60 percent in the early stages. If you have any problem with your sight, no matter how little it may seem, it is best to see your doctor.

Early detection is the key, so don't hesitate to have a checkup even if you don't have any symptoms. People with diabetes are also at greater risk for cataracts (a condition in which the lens clouds up and looks milky), open-angle glaucoma (the most common form of glaucoma), and neo-vascular glaucoma (which mainly appears to affect people with diabetes). Teens with Type I diabetes and poor glucose level control can develop "snowflake" or metabolic cataracts. This problem is frequently improved by carefully controlling glucose levels. Glaucoma is caused by increased pressure within the eye, which, if left untreated, can damage the back of the eye. This damage, in turn, will cause vision loss, headaches, and eye pain. Open-angle glaucoma is commonly treated with medical or laser surgery and usually results in a decrease in pressure within the eye and normalization of vision. Open-angle glaucoma is a disease that usually occurs in older people. The older you are and the longer you have had diabetes, the greater your chances of developing this disease. Neovascular glaucoma is a very severe form of glaucoma, which usually develops in people who suffer from severe diabetic retinopathy. This disease can be treated with laser surgery if discovered early enough.

All of these diseases can be treated if detected early enough. Don't wait until you have a problem to see an ophthalmologist or retinologist. Remember, warning signs don't always occur with these eye diseases, so make certain that an eye specialist is a part of your health care team.

Diabetes and Your Teeth

Diabetes does not cause cavities, nor does it increase your chances of having cavities. But people with diabetes are more prone to gum disease or periodontal disease if their glucose levels are not relatively stable. Remember, high glucose levels make it more difficult for the body to fight infection. Periodontal disease can cause gum loss and eventually tooth loss. Smoking also increases the risk of periodontal disease. Tooth loss makes it difficult to chew food and thus may discourage proper nutrition. Teeth that come out as a result of periodontal disease cannot be replaced. Because periodontal disease damages the gums, dentures will not be able to fit properly, and again this will discourage proper dietary habits. It is very important to maintain good dental hygiene at home by brushing and flossing daily and to have REGULAR DENTAL CHECKUPS at least every six months.

Diabetes and Your Kidneys

Diabetics of either type are more prone to kidney and bladder infections than other people. This can cause tissue damage to the kidneys over a period of time. This is called *diabetic nephropathy* and can lead to end-stage renal disease. End-stage renal disease means that a person's kidneys have lost their ability to function. A person with end-stage renal disease needs to have kidney dialysis or a kidney transplant to stay alive. In the United States, people diagnosed with end-stage renal disease often have diabetes. High blood pressure increases the chances of developing this disease. If you have Type II diabetes and smoke cigarettes or have high cholesterol, you further increase your risk for this disease. Controlling your blood sugar and your blood pressure as well as practicing good health habits can prevent or delay kidney complications. In addition, any urinary tract infection should be treated immediately. Your doctor should perform a urinalysis every year to determine the potential for this disease. At present there is no cure for end-stage renal disease.

Diabetes and Your Feet

Diabetes can damage the nerves in your feet and legs and cause problems with the blood flow in these areas. So it is very important to take extra care of your feet and legs. Wash your feet with warm water and soap, taking care to wash between the toes as well. Dry your feet especially between the toes. Don't forget to check between the toes. This is where athlete's foot grows. Use a lotion on dry skin (but not between your toes!) Change your socks every day. Also wear flip-flops in the gym or in public swimming pools. Always wear shoes and never go barefoot. Check the insides of your shoes before you put them on. That way you won't accidentally cut yourself on a pebble or something that found its way into your shoe.

Avoid anything that can restrict circulation, such as crossing your legs or wearing tight shoes or stockings. If you have an ingrown toenail or a corn or callus, go to a podiatrist so he or she can properly treat your feet. Check your feet and legs every day for cracks in the skin or cuts or sores. If something looks unusual, don't hesitate to call your health care provider or podiatrist. Smoking cigarettes increases the risk of damage to the nerves in the feet. If the nerves in your legs or feet are damaged you may not be able to feel a cut or sore there, and it could get worse. Infections and poor blood flow are the major reasons for amputations.

Diabetes and Your Nerves

Diabetes can cause changes in the nervous system (neuropathy). These changes may feel like a tingling or a buzzing. Hands and feet may become numb. A person may not be able to tell the difference between hot and cold. Or the person may not detect any changes. As with most other diabetes complications, diabetic neuropathy risk increases if a person has poor blood glucose control, smokes, drinks alcohol, or has hypertension. You can lessen your chances of developing diabetic neuropathy by maintaining a healthy weight, exercising regularly, not smoking, and keeping your diabetes under control.

Diabetes and Your Heart

People with diabetes face an increased risk of developing heart problems. High glucose levels contribute to the risk of heart disease by increasing the potential for clogged arteries, which then limits blood flow to the heart. The risk of heart disease increases even more if you smoke, have high blood pressure, and have high cholesterol levels. You can lessen your chances of developing heart disease by eating a balanced diet, maintaining a healthy weight, exercising regularly, not smoking, and keeping your diabetes under control. Your doctor should check your blood pressure at each visit. Remember, balancing a healthy diet and exercise can help control your glucose levels as well as your blood pressure and cholesterol.

Diabetes and Your Skin

If your diabetes is not controlled properly, you may become dehydrated, causing your skin to become very dry and itchy. Try using a lanolin-based cream or a moisturizer. If you are having trouble controlling your diabetes, you need to watch out for skin infections. High blood glucose levels interfere with the action of bacteria-fighting cells. If you get a sore or a small cut, treat it immediately. Keep the area clean and watch it. If it does not heal within ten days, call your doctor. You may need an antibiotic.

WHY ME?

Diabetes can affect anyone at any time. An average of 600,000 people are diagnosed with diabetes every year; most of them have Type II. There are more than 500,000 people in the United States with Type I diabetes and 30,000 new cases are diagnosed each year. Those are only the people who are diagnosed, but not everyone who has diabetes knows he or she has the disease. In June 1997, the ADA issued new guidelines for determining who has diabetes and said that if all Americans over the age of forty-five were tested for Type II, about 2 million would be diagnosed as having the Type II disease.

Diabetes and Your Family

If someone in your family has diabetes, it does not mean that you will get it as well. People can get diabetes even if no one in their family has ever been diagnosed with it. In fact, more than 80 percent of the young people diagnosed with Type 1 diabetes are the first in their families to have it. Scientists do not know the reasons for this. They do know that if your mother has Type I diabetes, you have a 1 to 3 percent chance of developing it. If your father has Type I diabetes, you have about a 6 percent chance of developing it. If both parents have it, your chances of developing Type I rise to 20 percent. Genetics play an important role in determining who is at risk, but scientists now believe that where a person lives is even more important in determining who gets Type I diabetes.

There is a stronger connection between heredity and Type II diabetes than Type I diabetes. About 5 million people in the United States have been diagnosed with Type II diabetes, and the ADA believes that the actual number of people with Type II diabetes is about 7 million. Native Americans lead the list on those most likely to develop Type II diabetes. They are followed by Hispanic Americans, African Americans, and then Caucasians. Lifestyle seems to influence the onset of Type II. People who are overweight, who have poor diets, and who do not get enough exercise are more likely to develop Type II diabetes than those who have a healthier lifestyle. But this is not always the case. Some people who eat a healthy diet and get plenty of exercise may still develop Type II.

Finland has the highest ratio of diabetes per capita of any country in the world, with the Italian island of Sardinia not far behind. The United States falls in the middle range. Scientists are looking for clues as to why people living in one place are more likely to get Type I than people living somewhere else. In the 1980s, researchers saw what they called a "pandemic" or a world epidemic of diabetes. Large increases in the disease were seen in places as far away as Poland, Japan, Sweden, and New Zealand, but also in Allegheny County, Alabama. So you can see that Type I diabetes can affect anyone.

Learning That You Have Diabetes

When a person is first diagnosed with diabetes, he or she will probably experience a wide range of emotions: anger, guilt, denial, depression, grief, and fear. You may have experienced all or some or maybe none of these feelings. None of these reactions are wrong. All of them are perfectly normal. These feelings can come in any order and return from time to time. These feelings become a problem only when they are not followed by acceptance and the desire to cope with diabetes.

Magda's Story

Magda was fourteen when she learned she had diabetes. At first, she didn't believe the doctor and her parents. "It's impossible," she would say whenever anyone tried to discuss it with her. "I'm only a kid. I don't deserve this." She refused to learn how to do glucose testing and give herself insulin shots. Every day was another battle in the house. Because stress aggravates diabetes, her blood sugar levels were always off. Finally, the counselor on her health care team warned her that if she didn't learn to control her diabetes, she would seriously endanger her health. It was time, the counselor told her, to accept the fact that many teens do develop diabetes. It was time to take responsibility for herself and to take control of her diabetes. The counselor gave Magda some "tools" to help her get through this crisis. The counselor taught Magda some stress reduction and deep breathing exercises to use whenever she felt so angry that she didn't want to do her SMBG (Self-Monitoring Blood Glucose) or take her insulin. Then the counselor put her in touch with a Teens with Diabetes Support Group in her area. By talking with other members of the support group, Magda learned that she was not alone in denying her diabetes. She also made a couple of friends in the group who encouraged her to call them whenever she felt as if she was going to give up control again. With the help of her counselor and the "tools" she had received, Magda began to take charge. Although she still resented having to take glucose tests and give herself shots, she found that after time it became almost second nature to her. And she started to feel better, her stress decreased, and her blood sugar became more stable.

The tools that the counselor gave Magda are available to everyone. Deep breathing and other stress reduction exercises can help you to relieve angry feelings that lead you to neglect yourself. Talking with teens in similar situations can also help you to understand your disease better and to recognize that others are coping. Contact a support group in your area.

Unfortunately, until a cure for diabetes is found, you will need to make a lifelong commitment to treating and controlling this disease. It's up to you to take control and not let your diabetes control you. Finding out you have diabetes can seem like just one too many things happening at once. You may experience a lot of different emotions when you find out that you have diabetes.

Anger and Guilt

It is okay to be angry. It's natural for a person who hears bad news to say it isn't fair. Or to ask "Why me?" Some teens feel guilty because they get diabetes. They think if they hadn't eaten all that candy or if they had eaten more fruit, they wouldn't have diabetes. No one thing causes it, and no one deserves it. Diseases are not punishments.

Denial

Denial is another common reaction. "Well, the doctors must be wrong. I couldn't possibly have diabetes. I just won't think about it." Although denial is a natural reaction, it is also a dangerous reaction if it goes on too long. Diabetes is generally not diagnosed until people are in their early teens, after they have had it for some time. It is important to find a way to accept that you have diabetes so that you can move forward and begin to take control of the care of it. That way you may live a long and productive life like many other people with diabetes.

Depression

Depression is another common response to being diagnosed with a disease. When you first learn that you have diabetes, you may feel very sad, almost as if you've lost someone important to you. In a way you have, and it's okay to grieve for that loss of the perfect self you thought you had. Yesterday everything was fine and today you have a chronic disease. But, as with denial, depression that lasts too long can adversely affect your ability to deal properly with diabetes and could have long-term harmful effects. You might want to try keeping a diary about your feelings. Expressing your feelings, whether in writing, in person, or by phone or e-mail to a parent, another relative, or a close friend can make it easier for you to cope with those emotions as they occur.

It is understandable that a person can get tired of having to do all the things that are required to control diabetes. There are so many things a person would rather do than monitoring blood glucose every day, eating a healthy diet, and exercising. But right now there is no cure and until there is one, no one can decide "not to be a diabetic anymore." If you do not try to control your diabetes now, you increase the risk of many diabetes-related complications and early death. There is no easy way around diabetes. It is up to you to keep your diabetes under control to have a healthy future. If you feel like you just want to give up, try talking to a friend or a counselor. Be open about how you feel. There is nothing wrong with feeling like giving up from time to time. The problem begins when you act on those feelings. By sharing these emotions with someone else, you can get a better sense of what you need to do.

TAKING CARE OF YOURSELF

Diabetes is not a simple disease. Remember that it is not really one disease, but several diseases. Diabetes is complicated, but the more you learn about it, the better you will be able to cope with it. When you were first diagnosed with diabetes, you or your parents were given some basic information and procedures necessary to survive on a day-to-day basis. That information included how to put insulin into a syringe, how to inject insulin, how to care for your diabetes equipment, and how to monitor your blood sugar and ketone levels with "finger sticks" and urine tests. You probably were given simple information on nutrition and diets. After you start taking control of your diabetes, you will find there is much more to learn, from simple hygiene needs to information about sophisticated equipment, such as insulin infusion pumps and oral medications.

Management

Monitoring Glucose: Finger Sticks and Urine Testing

Testing is important because you need to know if your diabetes is being controlled. When blood sugar levels are too high and insulin is too low, the cells are not getting the fuels they need to function properly. As a young person, you need your cells to function as close to normal as possible in

27

order to maintain normal growth and development. Monitoring your blood sugar and ketones is one way to help yourself. Finger sticks and urine tests are short-term tests. That means the tests give you an indication of what is happening right now. The tests cover a short period of time. You should do SMBG at least four times a day to ensure that you are controlling your diabetes.

The two short-term tests you should do are the finger stick and the urine test. Both of these you can do yourself at home or at school.

Finger Stick Test
The finger stick test involves pricking yourself with a finger sticker, or lancet, to get a drop of blood. This blood sample is then compared to a chart or it is inserted into a machine called a glucose monitor. Both of these methods will determine your glucose level.

Take readings in sequence before meals and at bedtime to tell if your blood sugar is following a normal pattern throughout the day. This also helps determine if you and your health care team have found the proper balance between insulin, exercise, and diet to suit your individual needs. The ideal is to keep blood sugar levels between 80 mg/dL and 180 mg/dL. The normal blood sugar level for a person without diabetes is between 70 mg/dL and 120 mg/dL before meals and less than 180 mg/dL two hours after eating.

Amelia's Story

Amelia had been diagnosed with diabetes when she was six years old. For the first year, her mother

How to do a finger stick

1. Wash your hands. This is always the first step toward any sort of health care procedure.

2. Stick your finger with the sticker and get a drop of blood.

3. Place the drop of blood on the testing strip and put it in the blood glucose monitor.

4. Start timing.

5. When the time is up, read the results.

6. Record the results. It is very important to record the results each time you perform the test. Don't rely on your memory. You could make a mistake. Also your health care team will want to see a record to assist them in helping you maintain the proper balance.

took care of all the testing and injections. Then Amelia began to take over the care of her diabetes. When she got to junior high school, Amelia found herself too busy to do as much testing as she had been doing. She limited her testing to just before bed, when she found some extra time. It wasn't long before

Amelia's diabetes was out of control. Amelia hadn't changed anything about her diet or her exercise or her insulin dosage, so she thought as long as everything stayed pretty much the same, all that testing was unnecessary. Her doctor explained to her that the growth hormones associated with the teenage years can cause dramatic fluctuations in blood sugar levels. Amelia learned that sometimes the fluctuations happen without any physical warnings. Her doctor reminded her that proper testing would let her know what her body was doing before it was out of control.

Being a teenager with diabetes means having to be extra careful about monitoring your glucose levels. Because the hormones associated with puberty can have a dramatic effect on glucose levels, it is possible to experience a rise or a drop in your blood sugar levels for no apparent reason. If you are monitoring closely, you will be better able to regain control.

Your health care team needs to review patterns of blood sugar levels to help you try to maintain the proper balance and to ensure that you are getting the proper amount of insulin. An occasional testing here and there won't establish a pattern, only a reading at one point in time. You always need to remember that what you do to control your diabetes today will have a great impact on how diabetes affects your life in the future. Daily monitoring of your blood sugar allows you to balance diet, exercise, and insulin before your levels get out of control. All sorts of things can raise or lower your blood glucose level, and if you are not testing for this, you are not in control of your diabetes.

Urine Tests

You use urine testing to measure ketones. You do this the first time you urinate in the morning. Urine testing is not as reliable as testing your blood. Urine tests rely on the "renal threshold." This is the level at which your kidneys begin to "spill" sugar into your urine. It is not uncommon in young people for urine to show high levels of sugar in the blood when in fact the amount is really okay for that person. Also urine tests only measure for "high" blood sugar and can't show "low" blood sugar (hypoglycemia).

The tests can show the following results:

- ↪ Negative Sugars, Negative Ketones: This means that your blood sugar stayed between 80 mg/dL and 180 mg/dL overnight. This is what you want to see.

- ↪ Negative Sugars and Positive Ketones: Negative sugars indicate that your blood sugar remained below 180 mg/dL overnight, but the positive ketones means you may have had a low blood sugar reaction while you were sleeping.

- ↪ Positive Sugars and Negative Ketones: This indicates that your blood sugar probably went over 180 during the night.

- ↪ Positive Sugars and Positive Ketones: This means that your overnight blood sugar went over 180 mg/dL and that your diabetes is out of control. Call your health care professional immediately.

Chemstrip K and Ketostix are the brand names of two commonly used ketone testing strips.

Urine Testing

1. Pass an unwaxed cup under the stream of urine to collect it. Or hold the stick or strip in the stream of urine, but make sure it is there for the right length of time.

2. Follow the directions for your particular kit, dipping either a stick or strip into the urine or putting a drop of urine on a tablet.

3. Wait the proper length of time.

4. Read the results and record them.

If you use insulin, you should test for ketones whenever you have two glucose readings in a row that are above 200 mg/dL. Both Type I and Type II diabetics should test whenever they get sick, get an infection, or experience extra stress.

It's natural to get tired of testing every day and to find the testing gets you down. It is okay to take a break now and then if you think it will get you motivated again. But you need to be careful. Don't decide to take a break from testing the same day you decide to go out for the football team or to eat an extra snack. Any change from your regular routine means that you need to test yourself so that you can modify your insulin intake to keep in balance. If you find that you need a break every few days, that's not good. Daily testing is something that is or should be a part of your life. It is something you must do every day to ensure your health. You can't just let it go. If you find it too much of a bother, you need to talk with someone, either a member of your health care team, a counselor, or someone you know who also has diabetes. While it is okay to skip a test now and then, it is not OK to skip a day or two. At the very least, you must test four times a day at least three times a week.

HYPERGLYCEMIA AND HYPOGLYCEMIA

What if your blood sugars are way off the mark? Is it your fault that you have bad blood sugars? First of all, when your blood sugar doesn't fall within the desired range, it doesn't mean that you are at fault. Nor does it mean that you have "bad" blood sugar. Try not to think in terms of good and bad. When your blood sugar doesn't fall within the desired range, it means just that: It is not within the desired range. The response should never be guilt; it should be to recognize that the proportions between diet, insulin, and exercise have to be redesigned to achieve balance again. Balance is always your goal, not guilt. Remember, the hormones associated with puberty can have an effect on glucose levels. It is possible to experience a change in your blood sugar levels even if you are doing all the right things. You may have to remind your parents about this as well.

Glenn's Story

I had been diagnosed with Type I diabetes when I was eleven years old. My glucose levels were pretty

33

	Hypoglycemia	Hyperglycemia
Other Names	Insulin reaction, Low blood sugar	Diabetic ketoacidosis, DKA, High blood sugar
Onset	Sudden	Slowly, hours or days
Causes	Too much insulin Not enough food Excessive amount of exercise	Not enough insulin Too much food or the wrong food Too little exercise Infection, stress
Symptoms	Sweating Headache Hunger Irritability Personality change Trembling Heart Pounding Blurry vision Extreme fatigue	Flushed skin Increased urination Loss of appetite, vomiting Thirst Weakness, stomach pains Ketones and high levels of glucose in the urine Coma
Treatments	Take a fast sugar or a glucagon tablet Call the doctor	Take fluids Take insulin Call the doctor

much under control until I got to be fifteen. Then all of a sudden, wham! They would go from high to low and back again for no apparent reason. My mom accused me of sneaking junk food. She just refused to believe me when I swore I was sticking to my diet. We'd fight about this every day. Talk about stress! Every time I had to take a reading, she was over my shoulder.

Glenn's story is common. The fact is that teenagers will have fluctuations in their glucose levels that have little to do with their diets. If your household seems like Glenn's, you may want to ask a member of your health care team to talk with your family. Your family needs to know that the teen years are a time when growth hormones surge through the body. These hormones can throw blood sugar readings off. If your glucose levels are so far off that you are in danger, you need to notify your doctor immediately.

Hypoglycemia

Hypoglycemia, commonly called low blood sugar or insulin reaction, happens when the blood glucose level drops below 70 milligrams per deciliter (70 mg/dL). It generally happens quickly. Hypoglycemia can happen for a variety of reasons that you may be able to control, such as too much insulin, not eating enough food, skipping a snack or meal, or engaging in a lot of unexpected exercise. You can avoid hypoglycemia caused by insufficient food or missing a meal by carrying a snack with you at all times. If you are in a position where you have no choice but to engage in extra exercise, be certain to check your glucose level as soon as you can. But hypoglycemia may occur for no apparent reason and you have no control over that.

If a person loses consciousness and cannot ingest food to bring his or her glucose level up, glucagon, available only through a prescription, can be injected to raise the glucose level quickly. Family members should be trained to be on the lookout for signs of hypoglycemia and know when and how to inject glucagon.

The symptoms of hypoglycemia are trembling, tingling lips, irritability, mood swings, sweating, hunger, fatigue, paleness, and loss of coordination. A person with hypoglycemia may also appear to be drunk. If you are with a friend who knows the symptoms, he or she won't make the mistake of thinking you are drunk when you are really suffering from hypoglycemia. But because you can't always be with people you know, hypoglycemia is another reason to wear a Medical Alert bracelet. If you are somewhere where you don't know anyone and you develop hypoglycemia, people may assume you are intoxicated and do nothing to help you. Worse, you could be in a situation where police assume you are drunk and arrest you rather than trying to help you. To treat hypoglycemia, you need a fast-acting sugar. There are several commercial products available that your doctor may recommend you keep close at hand. Hypoglycemia can also be treated with some fruit juice, raisins, hard candy, or a couple of Life Savers®. The benefits of the commercial glucose tablets are that they work faster than candy, have fewer calories, and usually contain no fat or sodium. Plus you probably won't use them to cheat on your diet. Also, because the dosage is specific, unlike being told to take a few pieces of hard candy, you are less likely to push your blood glucose level up too high.

Hyperglycemia
Hyperglycemia is also called DKA, diabetic coma, or high blood sugar. It comes on slowly as a result of rising blood sugar levels. The symptoms are fatigue, extreme

thirst, and frequent urination. When ketones begin to develop, you may feel nauseated and start to vomit, you may have stomach cramps, and your breath may smell sweet. Some of the causes of hyperglycemia, such as forgetting to take your insulin or eating too much of the wrong foods, can be prevented. Hyperglycemia is treated by adjusting insulin intake. If you notice any of these symptoms, check your glucose levels immediately. Sometimes people near you can smell the sweetness in your breath. Some people say it has a "fruity" smell. If someone mentions this to you, act immediately and monitor your glucose. Like hypoglycemia, hyperglycemia may occur no matter what you do. Hyperglycemia can develop into coma if it is not caught in time. The best prevention is to monitor your glucose levels regularly, especially if you are not feeling well.

Tight Control of Diabetes

Most people with diabetes follow a "conventional" approach to maintenance. That means that they test a couple of times a day, use the same insulin dosage each day, and see their doctor about four times a year. Tight control means more of everything. It means testing, at the very least, four times a day and adjusting insulin dosages accordingly, which means injecting insulin several times a day (Multiple Daily Injections or MDI) or using an insulin pump.

In the 1980s, the National Institutes of Health (NIH) began a study called the Diabetes Control and Complications Trial or the DCCT. The purpose of the study was to determine if people with diabetes who could keep their blood glucose levels within normal ranges or near normal ranges could postpone or avoid future diabetes-related complications. When the study ended in 1993, the conclusion was a resounding Yes. People with diabetes who can keep their blood glucose levels within normal ranges or near normal ranges can postpone or avoid future diabetic complications.

How Tight Control Works

Tight control is also called intensive therapy. Intensive is the key word. Intensive therapy is meant to help a person with diabetes have a steady supply of insulin similar to that of a person without diabetes. Although practicing tight control over diabetes is a lot of work, it actually gives a person more freedom. Because the insulin is delivered in very small amounts, it can be adjusted to match a change in activity or diet. People who practice conventional therapy have to adjust what they are doing to match the insulin they have taken. Whether the person uses MDI or an insulin pump to control the amount of insulin, he or she must monitor blood glucose levels often, adjust insulin dosages, maintain good records, and follow healthy diet and exercise guidelines. If you think you want to practice tight control, talk with your health care team and they can work out a plan for you. Tight control is a lot of work, so you may want to start slowly. You could begin right now by doing more frequent SMBGs and then working into MDIs. But you need to know that if you begin intensive therapy, you will probably gain some weight. In the DCCT study people gained an average of ten pounds. Also, with intensive therapy, you do not have reservoirs of insulin to tap into in case of low blood sugar, hypo-glycemia. So you need to be aware of the symptoms and be prepared to treat them.

If you have Type II diabetes, the keys to tight control are diet and exercise. You don't have to monitor your blood glucose levels as frequently, maybe only once a week or once a day. Remember, if you have Type II diabetes, your body does not use insulin efficiently, so glucose remains in your bloodstream. Exercise helps lower glucose levels.

You are probably unprepared to practice tight control if you are still angry or depressed about having diabetes or if you are not willing to become an active member of your health care team and do all the necessary testing and record-keeping. If you are not ready, maybe you will be later on.

Medications

Insulin

People with Type I diabetes have to take insulin. When Dr. Gilchrist received the first insulin treatment, it was very short acting and had to be re-administered frequently. Today you have better options. As with all types of med-ication, there are different types of insulin. There are more than thirty types of insulin. Animal-based insulin comes from purified pork insulin and purified beef insulin. Animal-based insulins last longer than human insulins but may cause skin dents (*lipoatrophies*) or swelling (*lipodys-trophies*) that human insulins do not seem to cause unless repeatedly injected into the same place. Lipoatrophies are

39

occurring less often today because insulin manufacturers take extra precautions to assure the purity of their products. Eventually all Type I diabetics will probably use human insulin, but right now it is not always available.

Types of insulin also differ in how quickly they act, how long they last, and how they look. You need to know not only the source of the insulin but its Onset Hours (how long it takes to get into the bloodstream and start working), its Peak Hours (how long it has its strongest effects in lowering blood sugar), and its Duration Hours (how long it stays in the bloodstream). There is unmodified insulin, which gets into the bloodstream quickly. Rapid-acting lasts six to eight hours. Unmodified insulin is clear and colorless. Lente insulin is made from beef, pork, or human insulin and contains zinc-insulin crystals. It reacts and looks like unmodified insulin, but it is used by people who have allergic reactions to unmodified insulin. Ultralente insulin is made from beef or human insulin and contains a lot of zinc, which causes the insulin to be absorbed more slowly and last longer than other types of insulin. NPH insulins are made from beef, pork, human, or a combination of beef and pork insulins. NPH insulins contain an ingredient called *protamine,* which slows down insulin absorption but increases duration. NPH insulins are slower acting than unmodified insulin. They are a cloudy, milky suspension. Protamine Zinc Insulins (PZI) last thirty-six hours or more and are also cloudy, milky suspensions. Human Insulin Regular is clear and colorless. It looks like water. Human Insulin NPH or Lente is uniformly milk-white.

All insulin bottles have a large letter or number on the

label that indicates the kind of insulin it is. Regular (**R**) and Semilente (**S**) Insulin act quickly (onset-hours). NPH (**N**) and Lente (**L**) are known as Intermediate Insulins. These insulins take a little longer to begin having an effect, but they last longer. Ultralente (**U**) is long-acting insulin, but it may depend upon the person. It takes even longer to start working than the other two types, but it lasts longer.

Most people use different types of insulin in order to maintain a consistent blood sugar level. Many people take a combination of insulins. $50/50$ insulin is half Regular (R) and half NPH (N). $30/70$ is another mixture. $30/70$ is a 30 percent Regular (R) insulin and a 70 percent NPH (N) insulin mixture. There are also other combinations: $10/90$, $20/80$, and $40/60$. The first number indicates the percentage of Regular (R) insulin. Remember, R insulins are fast-acting. The second number indicates the percentage of (N) intermediate-acting insulin. A 10/90 mixture means that the insulin is 10 percent R and 90 percent N insulin. These combinations allow the user to have fast action that lasts longer than if they just used one or the other. Lente (**L**) insulin is an intermediate-acting insulin that is made from 3 parts Semilente (**S**) to 7 parts Ultralente (**U**). Some insulins have other ingredients added to them to help prevent infections or to help them work longer. These additives affect how the insulin will work for you. Be certain to use the brand name, and not just the type, of insulin your doctor prescribes.

Your doctor will determine what kind of insulin works best for you depending on how much insulin your body produces, your diet, and your exercise habits.

Today the major manufacturers of insulin are Eli Lilly Company and Novo-Nordisk.

Types of Insulin	Onset Hours	Peak Hours	Duration Hours	Name
Short-acting	–	1 - 3	5 - 7	Regular (**R**) Semilente (**S**) Insulin Lispro
Intermediate-acting	2 - 4	4 - 14	18 - 24	NPH (**N**) Lente (**L**) Human Ultralente(**U**) *depends on the person
Long-acting	14 - 24	minimal	10 - 36	Human Ultralente(**U**) *depends on the person

Measuring Insulin

Insulin used to be measured by how much was required to change the blood glucose level in a rabbit. Today the method is more sophisticated. Now insulin weight is based on a crystallized sample and it is measured in **units**. When you buy insulin, the label on the bottle tells you how many units of insulin are in a cubic centimeter or cc. (A centimeter is as wide as your little finger nail.) This is called the concentration level. In the United States, the concentration level is almost always 100. That means there are 100 units of insulin per cc. On the label it is written U-100. Syringes are usually marked in units of 1 cc. If you use a U-100 syringe and fill it with insulin, you are using 100 units of insulin or 1 cc. If you fill it half way, you are using 50 units or 1/2 cc of insulin.

Rules

⮑ Always check the expiration date on the bottle. NEVER BUY OUTDATED INSULIN. Don't buy more insulin than you can use before the expiration date. NEVER USE OUTDATED INSULIN. Do not freeze insulin.

⮑ Although it is unnecessary to keep insulin in the refrigerator, it is a good idea to keep it cool by storing it in the refrigerator. If you do not refrigerate your insulin, store it in a place free from excessive cold or heat. But don't store your insulin at room temperature.

⮑ Don't shake the vials; roll them to mix the ingredients.

⮑ Make sure the ingredients look the way they are supposed to. Regular insulin is clear. If it is cloudy or has particles in it, don't use it. If your insulin is supposed to be colorless, and it has a yellow tint, don't use it. Lente and NPH insulins look cloudy. If you see solid white particles stuck on the vial after you've rolled the vial, don't use it. If you see clumps of particles or crystals in the insulin, don't use it.

⮑ Write down the name or type of insulin that you use, the species (beef, pork, or human), the company that makes it, the concentration (U-100), and the dosage. Memorize this. Keep a copy of it in your wallet or purse so that it's always handy. If you change types of insulin or dosages, remember to change this information on all your medical records.

There are a variety of factors to consider before you decide what type or types of insulin you are going to use. Your lifestyle is a very important factor. As a teenager, you probably are very active and on the go a lot of the time. You want to try one or the other or a combination. Your health care team will assist you in making a decision that is right for you.

When to Take Insulin

You should set up a schedule to take your insulin at the same time or times every day. Because every one is different, there is no definite rule about when to inject insulin. Your doctor or diabetes educator will help you decide when is best for you. It may be frightening, especially if you are afraid of needles, to think about injecting yourself with a syringe everyday. With some time and practice, it won't be so frightening. Your doctors will help you inject insulin so that it is a relatively painless procedure.

If you are on a regular schedule, you reduce the risk of forgetting to inject your insulin. If you forget, as soon as you remember, test your blood glucose level and call a member of your health care team for advice.

Injecting Insulin

Insulin is injected because the digestive juices destroy it if it is taken orally. It is injected through the skin, not into a vein. Scientists are working on insulin inhalers and insulin eye drops, but right now the results are mixed. Some people inject insulin using a syringe, some people use an insulin pen injector, and others use a pump that automatically injects it.

If you inject insulin, you should ALWAYS have this equipment readily accessible:

1. Insulin

2. Syringe and needle

3. Alcohol and sterile cotton

4. Glucagon in case of an emergency

5. Test strips

6. Medical identification

You should also change the site of the injection from time to time. Continually injecting into the same place can cause little lumps called *lipodystrophies,* also known as insulin-induced hypertrophy. Dents called *lipoatrophies,* also known as insulin-induced atrophy, can occur as well. Dents and lumps can also occur if you use impure animal-based insulins made from beef or pork. These lumps and dents are harmless, but you can lessen your chances of getting them by rotating your injection sites. One possibility is to keep a different site for injections at different times. Make a rotation chart for injections. Some places most commonly used are the outer area of the upper arm; just below the hip bone in the upper buttock; above and below the waist avoiding a two-inch circle around the navel; and the middle front of the thigh. You could use your thigh in the morning and your abdomen in the evening. Develop your own combination of injection sites for your chart. This way, while you are lessening the chances of lumps or dents, you are also maintaining a routine so that you know the timing and action of the insulin better than if you randomly changed the site daily.

Also remember when you are injecting insulin just before physical activity, don't inject it into the area you will be using the most. In other words if you are going to be running, don't inject insulin into your leg. It will absorb much faster than you are used to. Always wipe the top of the insulin vial with alcohol before you stick the needle in. Recap the needle when you are done. If you are using a "coated" needle, do not wipe it with alcohol. The needle has a special coating that makes injections easier, and alcohol will remove this coating. As long as the needle has touched nothing but the vial and the injection site, you can use the needle again. Do not reuse the needle if you are mixing insulins or if it has touched anything other than the vial and the injection site. If your needles are not coated, you can sterilize them by boiling them. If you have questions about reusing needles and syringes, ask a member of your health care team for advice.

Type II diabetes and medications

The most common therapy for people with Type II diabetes is diet and exercise therapy. For some people, however, diet and exercise are insufficient to control their blood glucose levels. In those cases, the patients are given oral medications. There are four categories of these medications: alpha-glucosidase inhibitors, biquanides, sulfonylurea drugs, and thiazolidiendiones. These medications may be prescribed alone, in combination with each other or other drugs, or with insulin.

The alpha-glucosidase inhibitor called *Acarbose* or *Precose* was approved by the Federal Drug Administration (FDA) in 1995. Acarbose lowers blood glucose levels by slowing down the digestion of carbohydrates.

The biquanide that you have probably heard about is called *metformin*. It was approved by the FDA in 1994. It is commonly sold under the trade name *Glucophage*. Metformin lowers blood sugar by helping the body to use insulin more effectively; it may work to help people with Type II diabetes lose weight and, consequently, have lower cholesterol levels. For some people, the use of metformin may eliminate the need for insulin injections.

Sulfonylurea drugs have been around for a long time. These drugs are divided into two categories: first generation and second generation. First generation drugs are the first drugs that are used to treat a disease. The trade names of the drugs in the first generation are *Diabenese, Glucamide, Ronase, Tolinase, Orinase, Oramide,* and *Dymelor.* Second generation drugs are usually stronger and have fewer side effects than the first generation drugs. You can buy second generation drugs under the names *Glucotrol, Diabeta, Glynase, Micronase,* and *Amaryl.* Second generation drugs are not always effective for all people, so don't discount your doctor's advice if he or she suggests you use a first generation drug. All of these drugs work by helping the body to produce more insulin.

The thiazolidiendione used by people with diabetes II is called *Troglitazone* or *Rezulin* and was approved by the FDA in 1997. This drug is similar to metformin in that it helps the body to use insulin more efficiently. It may also help a person with Type II diabetes to   stop taking insulin or to take less of it.

Your doctor and your health care team can help you determine which drug or drugs are best for you. Each medication has different side effects. One drug may be more effective for you than another.

If your doctor recommends that you try any of these drugs, remember that you still have to maintain your diet and exercise balance. None of these medications is a cure! Remember, the most common way doctors treat Type II diabetes is through diet and exercise. In fact, if you take oral medication for Type II diabetes and you regularly exercise and watch your diet, there may come a time when you no longer need medication. But never stop your medication without your doctor's advice.

Diet and Exercise

Diets for people with diabetes have changed a lot. In 1796, Dr. John Rollo's diet for people with diabetes was rancid milk, pork, suet, and bread. By the 1800s, people were told to take antimony—an element that induced vomiting and diarrhea. In the late 1800s, Dr. Arnoldo Cantani told his patients to fast every other day. Fortunately, things have changed a lot. The days of the "diabetic diet" are almost gone.

The fundamental key to good health for anyone is a good diet. This is especially true for people with diabetes. Although you can still eat the things you like, you must do so in moderation. Remember that part of everything you eat is turned into glucose. Because your body doesn't produce or use insulin effectively, you must be very careful to balance the amount of glucose you have and the amount of insulin you take. If you have Type II diabetes, diet may be your main means of controlling the disease. "Tight control" for people with Type II diabetes requires conscientious weight control. If you are seriously overweight, you need to eat low-calorie foods with high nutritional value to bring your weight back to a healthy range.

Take your diet seriously. According to the American Diabetes Association most people with diabetes do not take their diets seriously. The purpose of a healthier diet in the life of a person with diabetes is to control the blood glucose level. If you start taking care of your body now, you lessen the risks of many diabetes complications later in life.

There are all kinds of ways to watch your diet. The following are three basic types of diet that most dieticians recommend:

1. Weighed Diet. With this type of diet, you have a specific menu with specific portions of specific foods. You have to weigh and measure all the foods you eat. Weight Watchers and many other weight loss programs follow the "weighed diet." It is not a bad idea to try this method out, even if you don't use the weighed diet. That big bowl of cereal you have for breakfast each morning is probably three serving sizes. You will be surprised at the difference between your idea of a serving size and a "real" serving size. Ask your dietician for a cookbook.

2. Exchange Diet. This type of diet is almost like the weighed diet. You still have to follow a diet plan in certain proportions, which means measuring your food. The difference is that you can 'mix and match' your food. If you are allowed to have 1 bread exchange at breakfast, you can have a slice of bread, a biscuit, or a cup of cereal. If your doctor puts you on an exchange diet, ask your dietician for an exchange list.

3. Free Diet. This doesn't mean you can eat whatever you want. The free diet means you don't have to weigh your food, but you are expected to follow basic nutrition guidelines.

Diabetes and Sugar

Contrary to popular belief, sugar does not cause diabetes. Doctors used to warn people with diabetes to avoid sugar in the belief that a simple carbohydrate like sugar would raise the blood glucose levels much faster than a complex carbohydrate like bread. Recent studies have shown that simple and complex carbohydrates have the same effect on blood glucose levels in about the same amount of time. The ADA has released new diet guidelines for diabetics that do not limit the amount of sugar. That doesn't mean that you can now eat all the candy you want. You must maintain your diet balance and remember that while simple and complex carbohydrates are absorbed at the same rate, they may not have the same nutritional value. Too much substitution of simple carbohydrates for complex carbohydrates could result in excess weight gain and loss of nutritional value. Remember that sugar is a carbohydrate, and too many carbohydrates can raise your blood glucose. It is not always easy to know what foods contain sugar even when looking at the label. Sugar is identified by many different names. Generally the names for sugar end in-ose, as in glucose. Carbohydrates are usually listed on food labels. Carbohydrate is the key word.

Diet and Type I Diabetes

The three kinds of food that a person with Type I diabetes can eat are divided into carbohydrates, proteins, and fats.

51

Carbohydrates

One hundred percent of a carbohydrate is turned into glucose. Carbohydrates are used for energy and have four calories per gram of weight. There are two kinds of carbohydrates: simple and complex.

Some examples of simple carbohydrates are candy, soda (non-diet), cookies, cakes, honey, and syrup. Some examples of complex carbohydrates are breads, potatoes, rice, cereal, pasta, vegetables, and fruit.

Proteins

Proteins are used to repair cells and help us grow. Proteins contain four calories per gram of weight. Sixty percent of proteins break down into glucose. Protein is absorbed slowly by the body. Proteins come from all animal sources: meats, fish, and dairy products, and from nuts. Proteins can also be found in some plants and in grain. If you are having trouble with your kidneys because of diabetes, your doctor may recommend that you cut back on certain kinds of protein.

Fats

Fat has nine calories per gram of weight, and only 10 percent of it is turned into glucose. Fat is another source of energy for the body but must first be turned into ketones before it can be used.

There are five kinds of fat:

Cholesterol

Cholesterol is not really a fat but is usually included in the list because it is similar to fat. Cholesterol has a very important relationship with fat because it is carried through the body in molecules of fat and protein called lipoproteins. Cholesterol is used by the body to build cell membranes and to help make certain hormones. Cholesterol is manufactured in the liver. In fact, all the cholesterol one needs is manufactured in the body. The other way to get cholesterol is from eating animal products such as meat and dairy products. You have probably heard that there are two kinds of cholesterol: good cholesterol (high-density cholesterol or HDL) and bad cholesterol (low-density cholesterol or LDL). The fact is that all cholesterol is the same. What makes cholesterol good or bad is what kind of lipoprotein is used to transport it through the body. High-density cholesterol is cholesterol that is carried through the body by a lipoprotein that contains more protein than fat. This lipoprotein is called High Density Lipoprotein, which is what HDL really is. HDL is called the "good" cholesterol because it not only carries the necessary cholesterol through the body to the cells, but it then takes the left-over cholesterol and carries it back to the liver where it can be broken down. The other type of lipoprotein is made up of more fat than protein and is called a Low Density Lipoprotein, which is what LDL really is. LDL is called the "bad" cholesterol because if there is too much LDL in the bloodstream or not enough HDL, the cholesterol still gets carried to the cells but the LDL drops its excess cholesterol in the arteries instead of carrying it back to the liver. Different kinds of fats affect cholesterol levels in the body in different ways by raising or lowering the level of LDL and HDL in the bloodstream.

Saturated Fat

Saturated fat usually comes from animals. The meat you eat contains saturated fat. Butter and whole milk are other examples of saturated fats. Too many saturated fats in a diet cause the liver to increase cholesterol production.

Monounsaturated Fats

Monounsaturated fats come mostly from plants and seafoods. Examples are olive oil and canola oil. Monounsaturated fats are actually good for you in moderation because they lower the levels of dangerous cholesterol in your bloodstream by increasing the HDL level.

Polyunsaturated Fats

Polyunsaturated fats are similar to monounsaturated fats in that they come from plants and seafood. But polyunsaturated fats lower not only the levels of LDL but lower the levels of HDL as well. Corn oil and safflower oil are examples of polyunsaturated fats.

Triglycerides

Triglycerides are another form of fat that people with diabetes have to pay special attention to, because high levels of triglycerides usually indicate a level of DHL that is too low or a level of LDL that is too high. Either one may mean increased risk of heart disease. Because a person with diabetes is already at risk, high levels of triglycerides may only increase the risk.

The ADA recommends that people with diabetes should follow these dietary guidelines:

1. Fats should be 30 percent or less of your daily calories.

2. Saturated fat should be 10 percent or less of your daily calories.

3. Protein should be between 10 and 20 percent of your daily calories.

4. Cholesterol should be 300 milligrams or less daily.

5. You should eat twenty to thirty-five grams of fiber a day.

Your health care team or dietician can help you and your family work out a meal plan that will work for all of you.

How do you know what you are eating?

New food labeling guidelines are quite helpful to people with diabetes. Look at the Nutrition Facts panel on the side of the food package. Check the Daily Values column that lists the percent of nutrients in that food. You want a food that has a low percentage of fats and cholesterol but a high percentage of fiber. If you have to monitor your daily intake of fat, the Nutrition Facts panel also gives you the total fat calories as well as the percentage of calories from fat. The ADA recommends that you should not get more than 30 percent of your daily calories from fat. Carbohydrates and proteins are also listed. Another thing to watch for is the serving size. What you may think is a normal size serving of cereal may actually be twice the product's serving size. Learn to weigh and measure your foods, especially if you have Type II diabetes. The teenage years are a time when your body is growing

So, what can I eat?

1. You should eat at least 6 starches a day. Bread, cereal, pasta, and potatoes are examples of starches.

2. You should eat at least 5 servings of fruits and vegetables every day. Add different vegetables to a salad. Take raw vegetables like carrots or broccoli for snacks. Fruit makes a good snack as well.

3. You can still have desserts, but remember that the key word is moderation. Eat dessert only once or twice a week. Take smaller portions. Split a dessert with someone else.

4. In order to keep your fat calories within acceptable limits, you can do several things. Use less. Use low-fat or "lite" salad dressings and sauces (don't forget to read the label to see what "lite" really means). You can use fat-free toppings. Use mustard instead of mayonnaise. Use jelly instead of icing.

5. Cut back on saturated fat by eating leaner meats such as chicken and turkey. Eat seafood. Use low-fat or skim-based dairy products.

rapidly, and teenagers generally need more food than adults do. The trick is to consume nutritious foods and not just "empty" calories—calories with no nutritional value.

Exercise

No matter what type of diabetes you have, your doctor will recommend that you exercise regularly. Exercise uses up energy, and energy comes from the glucose in your blood. Twenty years ago doctors were reluctant to allow their patients with diabetes to participate in athletic activities. Today doctors and other health professionals are aware of the benefits of exercise. Not only does exercise help make you feel better by releasing endorphins, "feel good hormones," but regular exercise helps control your weight, tone your muscles, and control your insulin levels. Studies show that regular exercise not only helps prevent Type II diabetes but may also help some people with Type II diabetes avoid medication. The key to exercise is consistency balanced with diet. Vigorous exercise every now and then is likely to do more harm than good. You have to make up a regular exercise schedule and stick to it. You also must remember to monitor your glucose levels before and after exercise so that you may adjust your medication accordingly. Remember too that exercise alone will not do the trick. Exercise must be balanced with a healthy diet in order to be effective.

Before exercising, check your blood sugar level because exercise tends to lower this. If your blood sugar is low or some time has passed since your last meal, have a snack before exercising. There are also times when exercising will increase your blood sugar level. If your blood sugar level is over 300mg/dL, you should either wait for the level to decrease or inject some insulin before exercising.

What kind of exercise is good for you?

If you take insulin, you must learn to recognize that different types of activity use up different calorie values. You need this information so that you can adjust your food intake accordingly. Excessive or extra exercise can leave you with too little blood glucose. You should be prepared for this by carrying a snack with you when you exercise. Test your blood sugar before you exercise; if it is low, you may have to raise it. If you participate in after-school sports and the coach calls for that extra practice, be prepared by bringing a fast sugar food with you. If you begin to experience the symptoms of low blood sugar, stop practicing and take care of yourself immediately. It is also a good idea to have a high-carbohydrate snack before you begin exercise. A healthy sandwich and a glass of orange juice would be much healthier.

Remember that exercise must be balanced with insulin. Exercise burns up extra glucose in the blood when there is a sufficient supply of insulin in the body. If insulin is not balanced with exercise, you may find your glucose levels rising after a workout. If you find that exercise raises your blood sugar levels, you may have to take more insulin or you may just have to forgo that extra practice and wait until your glucose level falls. With a little practice you will be able to find that right balance of exercise and insulin that will work for you.

You should try to perform some form of exercise at least three times a week. The most basic and simplest form of exercise is walking. You could arrange to do aerobics with some of your friends several times a week. Or you might want to join a gym. If you use insulin, you want to be sure to tell your doctor about the types of exercise you do, especially active sports, such as football, cheerleading, or gymnastics. This way, he or she can make certain that additional calories are added to your diet to keep your glucose levels from dropping too low. Remember that your goal is to balance diet, exercise, and insulin. You cannot neglect any part of this balance if you want to control your diabetes.

Tests and Equipment

This section focuses on the equipment you will need to use to monitor and control your diabetes. The different kinds and brands of equipment, how they work, how to maintain them, and what to look for when buying equipment are discussed.

Some finger stickers, or lancets, are used only for sight reading; others can be read by machine and sight; and others can be read only by machine. Not all lancets fit all machines, so make sure if you have a machine that you are getting lancets that will fit it. Some machines are shaped like large markers. Others are shaped like powder compacts. Some lancet names are: B-D Micro-Fine Lancets, EasyStick, E-Zlets, Monoject, SoftTouch, Sugar System, Surelet, and Unilet-Lite. Some types of lancing machines are: B-D Autolance Glucolet, Dialet, ExacTech, Monoject, Pen-lt, and Soft Touch.

Glucose Monitors

Glucose monitors are small enough that you can carry them in your pocket or purse. They run on batteries and only take a few minutes of your time. But like every kind of machine, you need to know how to operate it properly. The FDA reports that many users of glucose monitors use

60

them incorrectly. In part, this is because many of the manufacturer's instructions are not very clear; also, the patient sometimes does not read the instructions carefully or does not consult the pharmacist or the health care provider for assistance. Here is what you should do if you are using a glucose monitor:

1. Make sure you have it calibrated correctly. If your initial setting is incorrect, then all of your readings will be wrong as well.

2. Read the manufacturer's instructions carefully. If you don't understand them, look for an 800 number on the monitor's packaging. Call the toll-free number to get in touch with someone who can walk you through the instructions.

3. Get professional instructions from your pharmacist, from someone on your health care team, or from someone who already uses the same type of monitor successfully. Don't take chances and unnecessary risks by trying to do something you are not familiar with by yourself.

4. Always use fresh strips and supplies and make certain you keep your meter clean.

Questions to ask before you buy a glucose monitor:

⇨ What is the cost of the meter and the supplies? If the meter is relatively inexpensive but the supplies are twice as high as those for other meters, it will cost you more money in the long run.

61

↝ How easy is it to get supplies? If the manufacturer cannot keep up with demand, you are left with a meter and no supplies.

↝ How much blood does the meter require?

↝ Is the meter easy to clean?

↝ Is it easy to calibrate?

↝ Is it easy to read?

↝ What kind of data management is required? Do you write your own record, or do you need something more sophisticated?

↝ Can you test it before you buy it?

↝ Does the manufacturer offer training in its use?

↝ What kind of warranty or guarantee does it have? Is there an 800 number you can call 24 hours a day? What kind of repair policies does the manufacturer have? Can you talk to some people who use this meter?

Glycosylated Hemoglobin Test

The Glycosylated hemoglobin test is called a long-term test. It is also known as the **Hemoglobin A1C Test.** This test is usually done every three to six months. It is a blood sample to see how much sugar coating is on a red blood cell. Red blood cells live approximately 120 days, and the sugar in the blood coats the cells. The more sugar in the blood, the more sugar on the red blood cell. Because the life span of a red blood cell is only about four months, an analysis of the blood sample gives a fairly accurate description of what the blood sugar range was over several weeks. Glycosylation is the sugar coating process that goes on in the bloodstream. Ideally, the results will show a reading about the same as for someone without diabetes.

INSULIN DELIVERY SYSTEMS

Syringes

Syringes are used to inject insulin into the body. Some syringes can be used more than once, but only if the needle is straight, sharp, and sterile. Do not reuse a syringe if the needle is bent. Always sterilize the needle before you use it again. Most plastic syringes are designed to be thrown away after one use. Glass syringes are meant to be used again, but remember that these instruments must be kept sterile and cannot be left lying around where others have access to them. You can sterilize glass syringes and nonplastic needles by boiling them.

NEVER use a syringe that is dirty. NEVER leave a used syringe lying around. NEVER simply throw a used syringe in the trash. Be considerate of others. Make certain you wrap the needle carefully so that no others, especially the people who take away your trash, accidentally stick themselves with it.

Make sure the syringes you buy match the insulin strength and dosage you are injecting. In the United States, the most common is U-100 insulin (100 units), so you would buy a U-100 syringe. If your syringe holds less than your dose, you will not be getting enough insulin. Make certain you can read the numbers on the syringe. If the unit marks are too small or too close together, you may want to obtain a different syringe. Some syringes have plungers that are different in color so that you can read the marks more easily.

Compare prices and pharmacies. If you find a cheaper price at a pharmacy far from your house, talk to the pharmacy nearest you. Usually they will match the price to keep your business. Always have an extra syringe on hand in case you break one.

Infusers

Some people use infusers to limit injections. With an infuser, a needle is placed under the skin and taped into place, insulin is then injected into the needle rather than the skin. Infusers must be changed every two or three days.

Pens

The pen is a new way to inject insulin. It uses cartridges just like an ink pen and usually costs less than $50. The pen is easy to carry and easy to use. Some are even disposable. You can carry an insulin pen right in your pocket. The pen contains a needle and an insulin cartridge. When you are ready to give yourself an injection you screw the needle onto the special end of the pen, make certain you have the correct dose (pens usually have a dial to adjust the dose), and then give yourself the injection. Not all forms of insulin are available in cartridge form.

Right now Lente (L) and Ultralente (U), the long-acting insulins, are not available for the pens.

Jet Injectors

The jet injector is a high-speed pen without a needle. The jet injector shoots insulin directly into you, under your skin. It is relatively painless and good for people who really hate needles. This is also a good insulin delivery system for those who have to take several shots a day. Jet injectors can cost up to $700.

Pumps

Using an insulin pump can greatly increase your freedom because, when used properly, it provides better control over your diabetes. Pumps are often recommended for people with brittle diabetes. Insulin pumps (insulin infusion devices) are also called open-loop systems. An insulin pump is about the size of a beeper. It is a plastic case containing a large syringe called a pump reservoir, a battery-operated pump, and a computer chip. The pump reservoir holds the insulin, and the computer chip is programmed to deliver a certain amount of insulin. Plastic tubing runs from the pump to the delivery needle (catheter needle). This is called the infusion set.

The needle is placed under your skin (subcutaneously), not in your skin, usually on the abdomen, but not where any clothing will interfere with it. Some people wear the pump hooked to a belt. Others wear it in a pocket. Women sometimes attach the pump to their bra. You wear the pump even when you sleep. The pump administers small doses of insulin all day long. The small doses of insulin are called the "basal rate." The continuous delivery of insulin keeps the blood glucose levels within normal ranges all day long and through the night. This continuous delivery of insulin helps control the "dawn phenomenon." The pump is programmed to give larger doses of insulin (a "Bolus dose") to balance out the amount of food eaten. Pumps are excellent for people wishing to maintain "tight control" over their diabetes. Because you control the insulin amount by simple programming, you can deliver different amounts of insulin without many injections. With a pump, you only have one injection every two or three days when you change the infusion set.

Although using a pump seems to make life easier for some people by avoiding several manual injections a day and by maintaining a steady dosage of insulin, that doesn't mean the pump relieves you of responsibility. In fact, while the pump allows freedom from giving yourself injections, it also comes with a whole list of responsibilities.

Before You Buy a Pump

Other things to consider before you buy a pump:

> ➥ Because your pump runs on a computer chip, you need to make certain the pump you are considering meets or exceeds Electro Magnetic Interference Immunity standards. This means that other electronic devices will not interfere with your pump.

> ➥ Make sure the pump you are considering has some sort of monitor that will alert you if insulin is not being delivered properly.

➷ Check to see if there is a safety range in the insulin delivery program so you don't accidentally set the program for an unsafe dosage.

➷ Get information about different pumps. Compare costs and benefits. Find out what kind of technical support the manufacturer offers. Check all the warranties and guarantees that come with the pump you are considering. Buying a pump that has a limited warranty is not going to be extremely helpful if the pump motor isn't covered. Read the fine print. Ask others who use the pump.

➷ Pumps are expensive. Some cost as much as $5000. Don't assume that your insurance company will cover the cost of one. Check first.

➷ If you have done all of your research and you are willing to assume all the responsibilities that go with having a pump and your doctor is unwilling to go along, ask another member of your diabetes health care team to intervene. If your doctor is not an endocrinologist or a diabetologist, he or she may not be as familiar with the pump as someone who is specialized in diabetes.

If you are considering using a pump, here are some things you need to be aware of:

➷ You must still decide with the advice of your health care provider how much insulin to program the pump to deliver.

↬ You must monitor the syringe that contains the insulin supply, the tubing, the battery, your skin, and your blood glucose levels. The major advantage of short-acting insulin is that it has a predictable absorption pattern, unlike NPH or Ultralente. The major disadvantage is that there is no "back-up" supply of insulin in your body if your pump fails. There is no emergency reservoir of insulin in your pump or in your body. When you're out, you're out. This puts you at risk for a quick slide into DKA (diabetic coma). Never begin a day without checking your reservoir and your blood glucose level. The syringe should be checked daily to ensure that you don't run out of insulin. Pumps use regular insulin, which is short-acting.

↬ You must change the infusion set every two or three days. This is an important responsibility for you.

↬ Most pumps come with an alarm that beeps if your battery is running low. If you hear this beep, don't wait until the last minute: replace the battery immediately. Know in advance how long a battery is supposed to last. Write the information down. Some pumps require that you send the battery back to the manufacturer for replacement. If that's the case with yours, make certain you have a spare. Make certain that the tubing remains clear and unbent. A kink in the tubing can impede the delivery of insulin. Make certain the needle is securely in place. And check your blood glucose levels often. Frequent testing ensures that you are aware of any problem before it becomes too big to handle.

↪ People who use the pumps are more at risk for skin infections at the insertion site. So make certain you check it daily. And make sure you keep your skin clean.

Living with Diabetes

Having diabetes will change many things about the way you live.

First of all, diabetes is a chronic condition that needs to be monitored and treated daily.

You will be responsible for monitoring your blood sugar levels and watching for ketones in your urine and keeping a log of all the results. You will be responsible for taking your insulin every day.

Second, you will be responsible for watching your diet and exercise so that they are in balance with your insulin intake. You will be responsible for saying no when someone offers you something you know will affect your diabetes.

Third, perhaps the hardest part about having diabetes at your age is having to assume so much responsibility for yourself. You probably are used to your parents taking care of you when you are sick. Your mother or father also decides when you go to the doctor and when you take medicine. Someone older than you is usually responsible for taking your temperature if you aren't feeling well. Now it is time for you to learn to take responsibility for your own health. Although you will have a lot of help from your health care team, you will be the main caretaker. Your health care team will rely on you for a lot of the information they will need to help you control your diabetes. Many choices about diet and exercise will be made by you when you are not at home. You will have to take the time out to take care of your diabetes and yourself. If you don't, you run the risk of extremely serious health problems as you grow older. Remember that what you do today will affect the rest of your life. There is no room for risk-taking with diabetes.

Fourth, you will have to make time in your schedule for doctor visits. You should learn more about diabetes so that you know what your health care providers are talking about. Make them talk to you, not just to your parents. After all, you are the one with the disease.

Learn to Accept Diabetes

Having diabetes is not an easy thing, and it requires you to change your life around, but it is something you must learn to accept even if it makes you angry at times. When you start to get upset, think about these questions.

What part of having diabetes worries you the most?

➭ Daily testing and injections?

➭ Feeling different?

➭ Diet?

➭ Exercise?

➭ Getting sick?

➭ Dying?

71

Let's take these one at a time and see if we can come up with some solutions.

If it's the daily testing and injections that are bothering you, you still have to ask why. Is it because they take so much time? Actually they take only a few minutes out of your day, so it can't be that.

Is it because the injections hurt? This may concern a lot of teens because many teens, and even adults, do not like needles. Sometimes the injections may hurt, but there are some things you can do to relieve that, such as rubbing the injection site with a piece of ice before you put in the needle. Also, it helps to pinch a large section of the site when you inject the needle. If one site hurts, try another. You might also ask your doctor if there is a topical anesthetic on the market that you can use to numb the area. You should also think how much better you feel once you have given yourself the insulin. If your injections continue to hurt, talk to your doctor or your diabetes educator. They may be able to tell you a better way to give yourself the injections so they do not hurt. You may want to try out different types of syringes to find the one that suits you the best. Today's needles have a special coating that makes those injections less painful. If the injections really bother you that much, you may want to consider getting a pump. But remember, having a pump means that you accept responsibility for testing several times a day.

If you are worried about how you are going to test and take injections at school, talk this over with your parents and your teachers. If you can, plan your testing and injections between classes. If that isn't practical, you can either perform the procedures in class or leave class to go somewhere else. If you are going to test and inject insulin in class, be certain to tell your teacher ahead of time so that he or she won't be caught by surprise. Try testing in your lap. Chances are no one will even notice. But if they do, remember it is normal for your classmates to be curious, at first. After a few times, this will all seem routine to them as well as to you, and no one will pay attention. If you prefer to test outside of the classroom, let your teacher know ahead of time that you will be leaving the class for a short time.

Are you afraid that having diabetes makes you different somehow? Remember that millions of people have diabetes. There are more than 16 million people in the United States alone who have diabetes. That is a lot of "different" people.

If your fear is really that people will look at you differently or treat you differently if they learn you have diabetes, it's possible that some people will. This can be especially difficult for teens. People you thought were your friends or schoolmates may not know anything about the disease, but they will make assumptions that may be hurtful. If someone makes hurtful assumptions or comments because you have diabetes, it shows he or she lacks knowledge about the disease and, more important, it shows a lack of sincerity. If this happens, turn to some friends who are sincere and try to talk it out. True friends will stick with you no matter what. True friends will be concerned and will try to make you feel at ease.

Are you afraid that you might not read the tests correctly or that you might give yourself the wrong amount of insulin? There are ways to prevent these things from happening. Practice reading the test strips before you give yourself an injection of insulin. Ask your diabetes educator to recommend test strips that he or she thinks would be good for you. Think about getting a glucose monitor that does the reading for you. If you are afraid that you are going to give yourself the wrong amount of insulin, remember that you and your health care provider have discussed dosages. You know how to match your glucose level and your insulin requirements with diet and exercise. If you still feel unsure, call your health care provider or get in touch with a diabetes educator to walk you through it again.

What else can you do to make sure you are getting the right dosage? Make certain your syringe is calibrated to match your insulin vial. Be aware of the symptoms of high blood sugar and low blood sugar. Do your SMBG at least four times a day. Learn to recognize when you need to adjust your dosage. Maintain a healthy balance between diet, exercise, and insulin. These things will come naturally to you over time. But if you've just been diagnosed, don't be afraid to call a member of your health care team for more information or reassurances. Get to know someone who has had diabetes for a while. Talk to that person and learn about his or her experiences. Ask lots of questions. There is no such thing as a stupid question. The more you know, the better you will be able to handle having diabetes.

Are you concerned that the diet is not what you will like or that you might eat the wrong foods? Diet doesn't mean just eating lettuce and rice cakes. There is no longer any such thing as a "diabetic diet." A healthy diet is one that has everything you've already been eating, but in moderation. You can still have a piece of pie now and then, but you have to balance your insulin intake as well. Your health care team probably includes a dietician who can help you plan healthy and delicious meals. Learn to read the Nutrition Facts Panel on food packages. If you have Type II diabetes, you MUST control your diet. Diet and exercise are the main methods to control blood sugar in Type II diabetes. If you are worried about going out to eat or how to deal with eating at someone else's house, there are some things you can do. You probably know ahead of time if you are going to a restaurant, so you can plan your insulin intake and exercise levels accordingly. Then as long as you don't go overboard, you'll have no problem. If going to a restaurant is a last-minute decision, you can order a salad or an appetizer and use that in place of one of your snacks. Ask for salad dressing or sauces on the side. Don't order fried foods. Remember to test your glucose levels as soon as you can. If you are invited to a friend's house, and no one there knows you have diabetes, again you will have time to plan for the meal. Eat small amounts. You don't have to eat everything that is put in front of you.

You may be worried about exercising, or you may just not want to exercise on certain days. Doctors recommend that exercise should be part of everyone's life, not just people with diabetes. Exercise can make you feel and look well and will ensure a long and healthy life.

One of the best exercises you can do is walking. Not only will it help keep your weight under control, but walking as well as other exercises help reduce stress by causing the body to release endorphins, the feel-good hormones. Again, just as with diet, you have to balance exercise and your insulin intake.

Are you worried about getting sick? It's normal to be concerned about getting sick, and that's why it's important to take precautions to avoid it. If you are worried about common illnesses such as colds and the flu, talk to your doctor. He or she will give you some common-sense rules about how to reduce your chances of getting sick. Remember, you should have a flu shot every year. But if you do get sick and have to stay in bed, there are some general diabetes sick days rules that you can follow. The most important thing to remember is to take your insulin, drink a lot of fluids, and get plenty of rest. If you are worried about getting sick as a result of diabetes complications, remember that you can help delay or even prevent many of the complications by starting to take care of yourself and to take control of your diabetes NOW.

Are you worried about dying? Before the 1920s and the isolation of insulin, if you were diagnosed with diabetes, you would die before the year was out. But the discovery of insulin has changed all that. People with diabetes live long, full, and productive lives, if they take care of themselves. Although it is normal to have worries about being a person with diabetes, too much worry can cause unnecessary stress. If you find you cannot stop worrying, you need to talk with your health care team about ways to minimize your worries. You might also want to talk to other people with diabetes to learn how they deal with their worries. Just as you can take control of your diabetes, you can take control of your worries.

Stress

Everyone knows that stress is a part of everyday life. But too much stress from worry, anxiety, depression, anger, guilt or even a physical ailment can increase blood sugar levels and lead to hypoglycemia. Stress releases additional hormones into the bloodstream that work to raise the blood sugar level in people. A person may not always be able to get rid of a source of stress. In that case he or she needs to learn how to cope with it and combat it. We tend to have some very recognizable physiological reactions to stress. We clench our teeth or our jaws. We breathe quickly and shallowly. We tighten our neck muscles and hunch up our shoulders. We clench our fists, grind our teeth, and sweat. We feel our heart beat faster. Learn to recognize these stress symptoms and work to reverse them.

Using deep breathing as an initial response to stress can help reduce its immediate effects. Gradually tighten and release all of your muscles several times. Take a moment away from the situation to "decompress."

Exercise is very helpful because it releases those good feeling hormones called endorphins. And exercise will help you keep in shape. That will also add to your positive self-image. Meditation exercises work too. Find a quiet place to sit. Practice some deep breathing. Then think only of pleasant things. If a thought you don't like crosses your mind, quickly think of something else. Meditation may seem difficult at first, but it will get easier each time you do it.

Diabetes and Males

Some complications caused by diabetes affect males

more than females, so you need to be on the watch for symptoms.

One of these is called *distal symmetrical polyneuropathy.* This complication can cause *sexual dysfunction* or impotence, the inability to maintain an erection. You increase your risk of developing this complication if you smoke, drink alcoholic beverages, or cannot keep your glucose levels under control. There is a tendency to think that just having diabetes will prevent a man from having an erection and, consequently, a healthy sex life. That is simply not true. Although some men with diabetes become impotent, others do not. So far, scientists have not established a direct link between diabetes and impotence. But some of the complications that develop from out-of-control diabetes may result in sexual dysfunction.

Out-of-control diabetes can inhibit growth. And because you cannot always control your glucose levels during the teenage years as well as you might want to, make sure your doctor measures your height at each visit.

After puberty, your insulin requirements may drop, so you need to monitor your blood glucose levels carefully so that you don't end up injecting too much insulin.

Diabetes and Females

Diabetes presents some different challenges to females that you need to be aware of.

Menstruation
If your diabetes is not properly controlled, your first period may be delayed. This is called amenorrhea, and it can

cause serious problems for you, not only now, but throughout your life. It is imperative that you begin to control your diabetes NOW. Proper diet and exercise along with insulin therapy can help normalize your blood glucose levels. Your health care team may recommend low doses of estrogen if you are over age sixteen.

Menstruation can raise and lower your glucose levels. This is partly because your body is releasing anti-insulin hormones. Because your body does not manufacture or use insulin the way someone without diabetes does, you need to compensate for this. It is common for young women to need ever-increasing amounts of insulin at night during the week before their period. Also, women who suffer from *premenstrual syndrome* (PMS) may be more prone to hypoglycemia during the week before their period. It is always important to follow your glucose level testing schedules but if you are prone to insulin fluctuations during the week before your period, testing your glucose levels often is very important. If your blood glucose levels tend to rise during this time, there are some things you can do:

1. Consult your health care provider about increasing your insulin dose during this week.

2. Watch your diet and avoid extra carbohydrates.

3. Exercise more.

4. Monitor your blood glucose levels.

If your blood glucose levels fall during this time, try the following:

1. Consult your health care provider about decreasing your insulin dose during this week.

2. Watch your diet and take extra carbohydrates.

3. Exercise a little less during this time.

4. Monitor your blood glucose levels.

Birth Control

Not all oral contraceptives are good for women with diabetes. Some may increase your blood pressure. Some may make you gain weight. Some may increase your blood sugar level. Be careful about what you take, and never hesitate to talk to your doctor about the side effects of medications.

Eating Disorders

Because people with diabetes have to balance their food intake carefully, being too thin is not an option. Unfortunately, young women sometimes have such poor self-images that they avoid eating (anorexia) or they eat and then vomit (bulimia) These eating disorders can make you very sick and may even cause death. Withholding insulin (also called insulin purging) is another related disorder specific to people with diabetes. By withholding insulin, a young woman immediately increases depression, which goes hand-in-hand with low self-esteem. She also places herself at risk of long-term disability or of dying young. If having diabetes has affected your self-image to the point of withholding insulin, talk to your parents and a trained therapist. You need support NOW. Don't think you can handle this by yourself.

Paula's Story

Paula was diagnosed with diabetes when she was fifteen. It was the end of summer and she had been preparing for the cheerleading tryouts for her high school, which were occurring in two weeks. It was a hot day and Paula started to get dizzy; then she just fainted. After some tests, the doctor in the emergency room determined that Paula had Type I and had fainted when her blood sugar went too low. The doctor immediately put Paula on an insulin regimen and put her and her family in touch with a diabetes health care provider. Paula was in the hospital for a week when she was released, she was told to keep her exercise levels down until her body could get back to normal. At first, Paula was angry that she could not try out for the cheerleading squad. It was something that she had been planning on for years. But her mother convinced her that it wasn't so bad; she could still try out the following year when she would be a junior. Paula adjusted to that with good humor. She started to take control of her diabetes. She learned to give herself insulin shots and to monitor her blood sugar. Her diet was already good because her family had always been health-conscious. After about three weeks at home, Paula noticed that she had gained several pounds. She began to cut back on what she was eating. When she did her SMBGs, her glucose level was always low. She lost some weight but continued to eat less than her dietician recommended.

Gaining weight can be traumatic if you are a teenager, but cutting back on nutrition is not the solution. If you have Type I diabetes and feel you have gained too much weight, talk to a member of your health care team. One of them should be able to recommend a combination of alternative foods and additional exercise. Cutting out necessary snacks or foods can put you at risk and is not the way to lose weight and control your diabetes. It is also not the way to reach your full growth potential. If you have Type II diabetes, you need to monitor carefully your caloric and fat intake and develop a good exercise program. Ask a member of your health care team to help you develop an exercise plan you can stick to.

This is your greatest growth period, and out-of-control diabetes can inhibit growth. In addition to working to control your diabetes, make sure your doctor measures your height at EACH visit.

Females also have to be watchful for *yeast infections.* These are recognized by vaginal itching and a white discharge. Yeast infections are caused by a fungus, *Candida albicans,* which flourishes on high blood glucose and moisture. Wear cotton underwear to decrease moisture. Sometimes you might develop a rash under your breasts. Your health care team can also recommend various powders and creams that will help keep rashes and yeast infections under control. As always, the first line of defense is to keep your diabetes under control as much as you can.

Diabetes and Sick Days

When you are sick with the flu or a cold or anything else, it's very easy to let your daily routine slide by. DON'T DO IT. When you're sick is the time to be very careful about maintaining your balance. Remember that in order for the body to repair itself quickly, it must have a steady supply of insulin. People who have diabetes do not have a steady supply of insulin and are at risk of more complications from any illness if they do not maintain a good insulin balance.

Always have your doctor's phone number close at hand. Let your doctor know that you are sick so that he or she can give you specific advice and medications.

If you take insulin, you must continue to take it just as you do every day. Not taking insulin when you are sick can cause serious complications and may bring on DKA. Your doctor may advise you to take extra insulin on those days that you are sick.

- Test your blood glucose levels at least four times a day.

- If you take insulin, test your urine for ketones at least twice a day.

- You need to eat the proper amount of food to balance your insulin intake. If you have difficulty keeping food down, take liquids, small sips at a time. Make certain the liquids contain carbohydrates if you are not eating.

- Drink plenty of fluids to prevent dehydration, especially if you have a fever. Write down how much you drink.

- Be careful of the medications you take. Aspirin can lower glucose levels. Check the labels for sugar and alcohol content.

- Rest.

Make sure your teacher knows why you are out, and make arrangements to have a friend pick up any school work and books that you will need to catch up.

Call your doctor (or go to the hospital if you cannot reach your doctor) if:

➪ Your blood glucose is greater than 225 mg/dL and your urine tests positive for ketones.

➪ You are vomiting and/or have diarrhea and you cannot take fluids.

You can decrease your chances of getting the flu by getting a flu shot every year. The Centers for Disease Control and Prevention (CDC) estimates that only about 40 percent of adult diabetics receive flu shots and that this percentage decreases considerably for younger people. Doctors at the CDC say that the failure to get a flu shot each fall causes thousands of people with diabetes to die from the complications of the flu. Having the flu is not just the same as having a cold. The flu is a viral respiratory infection that can lead to pneumonia. The flu can be very dangerous even for people who do not have diabetes but especially for those who do have chronic diseases such as diabetes. Remember, high blood glucose levels impair the body's ability to fight infection.

Diabetes and Your Teenage Years

The teenage years are a time of experimentation. For someone with diabetes there is no room for experimentation with anything that can alter your glucose levels or affect your health. You may be invited to a party where other kids are drinking or taking drugs. It's not always easy to "Just Say No," especially when you're with your friends or people you want to impress. But by saying yes to drugs or doing something that you know will affect your diabetes, you are endangering your health.

Drinking and Diabetes

If you have diabetes, alcohol can be dangerous to you. Alcohol is full of calories. It has double the calories per gram that fat does. Beer and most mixed drinks contain carbohydrates. Although drinking beer will initially raise your glucose levels, if you drink on an empty stomach your blood sugar could drop very quickly and you may go into a diabetic coma. This is because your liver cannot process alcohol and release glucose at the same time. It can't do both very well at the same time. Also many diabetes medicines warn that mixing alcohol with the medicine could cause serious problems. Another thing to remember is that a person experiencing hypoglycemia can appear to be drunk to others. If you are drinking at a party and go into DKA, your friends may just think you've had too much too drink and not recognize that you are sliding into hypoglycemia. If you have Type I diabetes you need to know that alcohol is poison to the nerves, and as a diabetic you are already at risk for potential nerve damage. Alcohol has been linked to the development of diabetic retinopathy. Alcohol is also harmful to the liver, heart, and kidneys.

So what should you do if you are at a party and alcohol is being served? You should just say you don't want any.

85

You do not have to explain. If someone insists that you have a drink, remember the dangers to yourself. Would a friend insist that you put yourself in danger? Of course not. If you have to say no again, do it. It won't be easy the first time, but after a while, it comes very easily.

Drugs and Diabetes

Drugs are dangerous for people without diabetes, so those who have diabetes face serious consequences to their health. Controlling your diabetes is the most important part of keeping yourself healthy. Drugs just get in the way of that goal.

➷ Cocaine raises blood pressure and blood glucose. Cocaine can cause irregular heartbeats and heart disease.

➷ "Diet pills" or "speed" increase the heart rate and decrease appetite. This can result in low blood sugar and can increase the chances of hypo-glycemia.

➷ Marijuana increases your appetite. It gives you the "munchies." If you break out of your dietary habits while you are on marijuana, your blood sugar will rise. Because marijuana can also cause lethargy, you may not care that your blood sugar is rising and thus do nothing to alter it. The result could be DKA.

➷ Tranquilizers, muscle relaxants, and sleeping pills slow down your breathing and can hide the signs of hypoglycemia.

It is not easy to remember to monitor your blood glucose levels when you are stoned, and that is a time when you need to be very careful. Using drugs or alcohol when you have diabetes is irresponsible and is not a way to take control of your disease.

Smoking and Diabetes

The teenage years are a time when most people begin to smoke. According to Liggett and Meyers, a cigarette manufacturer, tobacco companies target teenagers with their ads. You already know about the dangers of smoking for people without diabetes. For people with diabetes, the dangers are even greater.

Smoking narrows the blood vessels and decreases circulation to the limbs. More than 90 percent of diabetic limb amputations are on smokers. Smoking also increases the risks for diabetics of developing heart disease, kidney disease, nerve disease, and eye disease. These are diseases that diabetics are already at greater risk of developing than are people in the general population. Nicotine, the additive ingredient in tobacco, contributes to heart disease. Tobacco smoke coats your lungs with residue that inhibits their ability to clean themselves. Weakened lungs make a person more susceptible to respiratory infections such as bronchitis. The carbon monoxide in cigarette smoke also cuts down on the oxygen supply to the body, making exercise more difficult. Smoking is addictive. If you smoke, stop now. If you are thinking about smoking, think again. If you need help in quitting, talk to members of your health care team NOW.

Junk Food

Because you are in a period of rapid growth, your body requires more food than an adult's. Your diet plan probably has several snacks scattered throughout the day. If you go out with your friends on the weekend or after school, you can use some of your snack food requirements. Not all junk food is bad for you. Like everything else, the key word is moderation. You can eat a slice of pizza or a burger but avoid having a bacon cheeseburger with a side of fries or onion rings. Pick one or the other. You can drink diet soda. Some fast food places have salads or salad bars. Don't feel that you have to stay away from your friends when they go out to eat. And, of course, you can always say no when you are offered something you don't want or know you shouldn't eat.

Other Areas of Concern

Going to concerts or the movies

First of all, you should always have some sort of fast sugar food with you. Put it in your pocket or in your purse. If anyone gives you a hard time, explain your situation. It would be helpful if you had a Medical Alert bracelet or medallion. If someone still gives you a hard time, ask to see the manager. There is no need for you to carry such massive amounts of food that it is obvious. Keep a supply in your pocket or bag. More often than not, no one will question you about it.

Traveling

Diabetes should not interfere with any travel at all. But you need to plan ahead.

Make certain you have enough medication with you. Don't pack it in a suitcase that might get lost. Make certain you have a copy of any prescriptions you may need. Carry fast sugar food with you. Remember, if you cross time zones, you need to adjust your medication accordingly.

If you are going to another country and have to have immunizations first, make certain you get them well enough in advance to allow any bad reactions to be alleviated. Know where the hospitals are. Know how to ask for a doctor. Know how to say that you have diabetes in the local language.

If you do get the flu, call your doctor. Be careful what medications you take. Decongestants can raise blood pressure. Some cough syrups contain sugar and alcohol. Follow your Sick Day Guidelines. Being sick increases stress, so be sure to monitor your glucose levels carefully so that you can adjust your insulin levels.

Telling Others You Have Diabetes

It is normal not to want others to know about your diabetes at first. You may need time to think about what having diabetes means to you before you share your diagnosis with your friends. But after a while, keeping your diabetes a secret becomes an unnecessary burden to you, your family, and your friends. Although you do not have to tell everyone you have diabetes, there are several groups of people you should tell.

You should tell your teachers and your school. You should let your school know that you have diabetes so that if you have sick days you will be able to make up your work without a problem. You should also tell people at your school so that there is not a problem when you carry syringes to school. You should tell your teachers so that they will be understanding when you have to test during class or when you need to give yourself an injection or eat a snack. Telling your teachers in advance will avoid problems later on. If your teachers are not understanding, you can have your doctor or another member of your health care team speak to them. You also need to tell your teachers so that they can be aware of the signs of hypoglycemia or hyperglycemia and be prepared to react to those situations.

If you are involved in sports, **you should tell your coach.** Because exercise has an effect on glucose levels, your coach needs to be aware of potential problems, just as your teachers do, so that he or she can react to them in time. If you are afraid to tell your coach because you think you will not be allowed to participate, you may want to talk to someone in the school administration first. There is no reason to prevent students who have their diabetes in control from participating in athletic activities. People with diabetes can be found in every type of sport today.

There is no real need to tell your classmates, but if you are testing during class, they will probably figure it out. Letting your classmates know you have diabetes and answering their questions about the disease is a good way to educate others.

You should tell your friends. You want your friends to know that you have diabetes for several reasons. Keeping your diabetes a secret from your friends means that you will have to waste a lot of time making up stories about why you can't eat that extra dessert or eat that free order of fries. Keeping your diabetes a secret means that you will have to keep all your testing supplies and insulin hidden while you are at school and when you are at home. Keeping your diabetes a secret means that if you get into trouble with your diabetes, no one will know what is happening, and worse, no one will be able to help you. Keeping your diabetes a secret will add to the stress in your daily life, and you know that too much stress is not good for a person with diabetes.

Another reason to tell your friends about diabetes and to explain to them what it means to have diabetes is because one of the signs of hypoglycemia is irritability. If you appear cranky all of a sudden when you are usually upbeat, a friend who knows about diabetes may be more understanding and may even alert you to the fact that you need to test your blood sugar. A friend may save your life some day.

If you are reluctant to tell someone about having diabetes, ask yourself why.

Are you afraid that person will not like you anymore? Sometimes it happens that someone you tell will begin to avoid you. There is not much you can do about that except to realize that person was probably not a good friend after all. While that may not make you feel better at first, later you'll see that you have friends who are loyal and whom you can trust.

Are you afraid that person will treat you differently if he or she knows you have diabetes? When you tell someone you have diabetes, you should also give that person some information about the disease. When you first tell someone, that person may ask all sorts of questions. That is a natural response. Answer the questions as honestly as you can. Be certain to let people know that having diabetes does not mean that you are a different person. Having diabetes means that you have to balance diet and exercise, not retire from your social life.

Are you ashamed of having diabetes? It is important to remember that diabetes is a disease that anyone can get. Diabetes does not mean that a person is good or bad. There is no reason to be ashamed. Having diabetes does not mean that you lose your identity. Do not let the fact that you have diabetes make you feel that you are somehow "different." You aren't.

Camps for People with Diabetes

There are many summer camps for young people with diabetes. Some of these camps are specifically for those who want to play a particular type of sport, or for those who live in a certain area. There are camps just for girls and camps just for boys. Ask someone on your health care team for some addresses or contact the American Diabetes Association for information on camps. At camp you will be with others who have almost the exact same problems you do. Camp is a good place to learn more about how others react in special situations. It is also an excellent place to make friends with people who already understand most of what you are going through. Sometimes it feels good just to be able to relax and not have to explain about having diabetes.

Dealing with Health Care Professionals

You will have not one doctor but several doctors because diabetes is a syndrome (a collection of several diseases). First you probably have a pediatrician, then an endocrinologist to check hormone levels and advise you and your family on various diabetes treatments. You should also have a diabetes educator to assist you in learning about the disease and to help you understand it better. A diabetes educator is the person to turn to with all sorts of questions you may have. A podiatrist will help you care for your feet, an ophthalmologist or a retinologist will care for your eyes. You will probably have other health care professionals as well, such as a dietician to help you plan a workable diet for your lifestyle, a psychologist to help you and other family members deal with the emotional stresses of diabetes, and a social worker to assist you and your family in finding community support programs as well as financial resources to pay for your treatment.

According to the ADA, these are things you should expect your health care team to ask each time you meet:

1. Ask for your blood glucose records. This information is important because your insulin may have to be adjusted at different times throughout the day to compensate for different glucose levels.

2. Ask about any life changes. Remember, stress affects diabetes.

3. Ask if you've made any changes in your care program or if you've had any problems with it.

4. Ask if you've been sick since your last visit. Again, remember that illness can affect insulin level and some illnesses may be related to your diabetes.

5. Ask what medications you are on. Different medications can interact with each other and with insulin. If your health care team has all of this knowledge, they can then make recommendations and substitutions as necessary to prevent complications.

6. Ask about your periods, if you are a female.

If these questions aren't being asked, volunteer the information. If no one seems interested, then it may be time to look for a different health care team.

These are things you should expect your health care team to do each time you meet:

1. Take blood for a glycohemoglobin test

2. Take a urine sample

3. Check your eyes

4. Check your feet

94

5. Check your weight

6. Check your height

7. Check your blood pressure

If these things aren't being done, ask why not. If no one seems interested, then it may be time to look for a different health care team.

There are other things you have a right to expect from your health care providers.

Your Health Care Rights

You have a right to be treated with dignity and respect
Sometimes older people tend to view teenagers as irresponsible and incapable of making good decisions. If any member of your health care team treats you with disrespect or doesn't clearly expain things, speak up. If you are unwilling to confront that person, tell another member of your health care team about it. Don't keep quiet and just worry about each visit with that person. That is just unnecessary stress.

Your doctor and each member of your health care team should talk with you about diabetes and your care. They should not lecture you. After all, it is supposed to be a team effort, and you are the most important member of the team. Don't forget that.

You have a right to ask questions and expect answers
Because you are not yet considered an "adult," you may

find that some members of your team are reluctant to discuss things about your disease with you. If you find that happening, you will have to become more assertive when you deal with those members of your team. If you are controlling your diabetes in a responsible manner, there is no reason why your health care team should not discuss all aspects of your treatment with you as well as your parents. Speak up if you are not being informed. Or ask your parents not to accompany you into the doctor's office. Be prepared when you go to the doctor. Have a list of questions written down. Check them off as the doctor answers them for you.

You have a right to have all procedures, tests, and medicines explained to you in language that you, not just your parents, understand

If your doctor is not explaining things to you so that you understand them, he or she is doing you a disservice. After all, you are the one who has diabetes, and you are the one who is mostly responsible for controlling it. If your doctor uses words that you don't understand, interrupt and say, "I don't understand. Could you please explain it to me in other words?" Don't worry that you may sound as if you don't know what the doctor is talking about. You don't, and you need to.

You have a right to information about the variety of available treatments

Some doctors are partial to certain kinds of treatment and not to others. That does not give your doctor or any other member of your health care team the right to withhold any information about different kinds of available treatment. If you have heard about a new treatment, you have a right to expect your doctor to discuss the good and bad things about it. If, after discussing a new treatment or procedure thoroughly, you and your parents decide to go ahead with it, you have a right to expect that your doctor and other members of your health care team will be supportive of your decision.

You have a right to privacy

There may be some things you need to talk to your doctor or other members of your health care team about that you don't want your parents to know about. You may have questions about birth control or drugs or how diabetes may affect your sex life in the future. Ask your doctor if he or she will maintain your confidence and not discuss your questions with your parents. Don't assume that confidentiality is the rule. You are still considered a minor and under your parents' protection. If your confidentiality cannot be guaranteed, then you need to find someone else with whom to discuss these matters. You may want to try a diabetes hotline or contact the American Diabetes Association for more information about the sensitive topics.

If you find that you and your health care team don't get along for any of the reasons above or because you just don't fit together as personalities, ask your parents about finding another doctor. It is important to get along with your health care team. You must feel comfortable when you are with any one of them. You must be able to trust their judgments and opinions. If you are not comfortable, you will always wonder if you are getting good advice.

Your Health Care Team and You

Just as you have a right to expect certain things from your health care team, they have a right to expect certain things from you.

They have a right to expect you to be honest about your testing habits and record-keeping. If you are only testing once or twice a day, don't tell anyone you are testing four or five times a day. You test in order to adjust your insulin dosage to your needs. If you are only testing once or twice a day, you are not adjusting according to your needs and you are not displaying a true record of your overall glucose levels.

They have a right to expect you to be honest about your eating habits and exercise. If you do not tell your doctor the truth about what you eat or how you exercise, he or she may make incorrect assumptions about your insulin adjustments. If you are reluctant to tell the truth because you don't want to seem irresponsible or you don't want your doctor to be angry, you are merely putting yourself at risk. First of all, if you do not follow your diet and exercise plan, you are not hurting your doctor, so he or she has no right to get angry. Second of all, if you are consistently breaking your diet and exercise rules, it may be that those particular rules are not good for you and your doctor may need to help you adjust them. However, if you are given several different plans and are unable to stick with any of them, maybe you need to ask yourself if you are being responsible or not.

You should be keeping a record of your glucose testing results. This should include the date and time of the testing and the results. You also might want to include any changes in your usual schedule that might have had an effect on your glucose level. You could draw a simple chart like this:

Day	Time	Results	Unusual Events

Or you may be able to get a free booklet from your health care team. There is also a variety of shareware software available on the Internet that you could use.

This record-keeping may also help you normalize your schedule. You will be able to see at what times of the day your blood sugar is too high or too low and be able to make adjustments to help you maintain the proper balance.

Your health care team needs accurate information in order to help you. If you are not keeping records of your testing and insulin dosages, don't make excuses. Chances are they have already heard the same excuse from someone else. Keeping good records helps your health care team understand how your body is working, but more important, keeping good records lets you know how your body is working and is one of the steps toward tight control.

How Will Diabetes Affect My Life?

Diabetes and Your Family

When you were first diagnosed, probably everyone in your family was confused about what having diabetes meant and how it would affect the family. A diagnosis of diabetes does change family dynamics and requires everyone to develop different coping skills. First a family must learn to integrate diabetes into their daily lives. The first step toward this is learning as much as you can about the disease. Your doctor and other health care professionals can give you a lot of information. There are also other resources such as the ADA and the Juvenile Diabetes Foundation (JDF). You and other family members may want to join a diabetes support group. The ADA has an office in every state which has a list of educational services and support groups.

If the diabetes requires insulin injections, both you and your parents have to learn how to do this. It can be scary at first, but usually all of you are allowed to practice with oranges and syringes or something similar. No one is sent home from the hospital with a syringe and some insulin and no training. Remember, you are not injecting anything into a vein, so relax. Everyone in the family should be taught the warning signs of hypoglycemia and hyperglycemia and know what to do in an emergency. Chances are the family diet may have to be changed to accommodate diabetes. The good news is that this diet is probably healthier for everyone. It is a good idea for your family to stop buying junk food for a while until you are in control of your diabetes. That way you won't be tempted and you won't feel resentful about what other family members are eating. You and your parents are going to have to learn how to share information with each other and how to ask the questions that you need to. Ask when you go to the doctor.

Second, but even more important, you and your family are going to have to come to terms with one another about wants and expectations concerning your diabetes. You cannot expect that your parents will immediately let you resume life as usual, and your parents can't expect that all of a sudden you have become a different person. You and your family may have to learn how to manage stress more effectively because having a child with a chronic disease such as diabetes or being the person with diabetes can increase the stress within a family, especially in the beginning. The family will have to learn how to adapt. A counselor may be needed and is almost always helpful to teach family members new ways of coping. Diabetes support groups are another resource where family members can talk about their problems and learn how other people in similar situations have handled them.

Family members must identify what is expected of one another. The parents provide positive role models by not eating a lot of junk food. You follow diet guidelines and expected patterns of behavior in order to balance your diabetes. Learn to identify the stresses within your family.

Your parents

Your parents probably experienced a lot of the same emotions you did when they learned you had diabetes: denial, anger, guilt. Your mother may feel she should have done something else while she was pregnant with you or she should have fed you different food. No one is responsible for diabetes. You may find that your parents are overprotective. They may take on the responsibility of monitoring and treating your diabetes. At the doctor's office, they may be the ones to ask the questions and get all the answers. While this is all right for the first few months after diagnosis, it is not the way for you to learn to be responsible for yourself. If your mother or father is talking to the doctors without you, ask that you be allowed to sit in. Remind them that it is your disease and you need to know all you can. Your parents may be afraid that too much information will frighten you or that you won't understand what the doctor is saying. You can remind them that the more information a person has about an illness, the easier it is to come to terms with it and control it.

Overprotective Parents

Some parents may be overprotective, not allowing you to do anything yourself, limiting your outings with your friends, constantly monitoring your diet and exercise.

Dennis's Story

My parents learned I had diabetes when I was twelve. I just couldn't get up for school one morning. I felt like I had the flu really bad. My mom took me to the doctor, who at first couldn't find anything wrong. Finally, he did a test that determined I had Diabetes I. My mom started to cry when the doctor told her. I didn't really understand what was going on because my parents didn't talk to me about it. But all of a sudden they started treating me differently. Every morning my mom would wake me up and monitor my blood sugar. She was also the one who gave me my insulin injections and kept the monitoring records. My dad kind of stayed away from me for a while. We used to play football on the weekends, but that stopped. It was like they were afraid I would break or something. I wasn't allowed to go on field trips with my class or go to the movies with my friends because my mom thought I would eat candy or something I shouldn't. It was awful. I started fighting with my parents all the time, especially with my mom. It was as if my life had stopped being my own when I was diagnosed with diabetes. I was a baby again. I snuck out with my friends whenever I could. I started eating more junk food than I ever did before to get back at my mom. She couldn't understand why my blood sugar readings were always off. She thought she was reading the results wrong, so she didn't adjust my insulin. One day I was out with my friends, and we went to this fast food place. I ordered a couple of cheeseburgers and an extra large milk shake. A little while later I started feeling sick to my stomach. The next thing I remember I was in the hospital."

Dennis was lucky he survived. Too little insulin and too much food, especially the wrong kind of food, upset his balance. He developed hyperglycemia and went into a diabetic coma. Fortunately, his friends knew he had diabetes, and one of them called his mom and an ambulance. It is not unusual for parents to become overprotective. It is also not unusual for children, especially teenagers, to react in the way Dennis did. Unfortunately, neither behavior is good for the person with diabetes or for the family unit.

By being overprotective, Dennis's parents were denying him the right to assume responsibility for his own care. Also his parents did not seem to understand that having diabetes does not mean that a person cannot live a normal life. Having diabetes means that you have to be careful to balance insulin, exercise, and diet. It does not mean that you cannot enjoy sports or eat some occasional junk food or hang out with your friends.

By taking unnecessary risks to get back at his parents, Dennis was denying the reality of his disease. He did not seem to understand that what he was doing would have a dangerous impact on his health. Dennis could have died if his friends hadn't known what to do. By behaving irresponsibly, Dennis was hurting himself the most.

Punishing Your Parents

Do you ever try to punish your parents by doing things that you know you shouldn't do? Most teenagers do. The important thing to remember is that if you are doing things that have an impact on your diabetes, you could do harm to yourself that you will have to live with for the rest of your life. Proper care for diabetes starts immediately. There is no time off!

104

Tanisha's Story

Tanisha was told she had diabetes when she was fourteen. Her mother promptly told every person in the family and in the apartment building where they lived that Tanisha was a diabetic. At first Tanisha was embarrassed. "Everyone looked at me like I had some kind of strange plague or something," Tanisha said. "People I used to hang out with started avoiding me. Everywhere we went Mom told somebody. And she started treating me like I was a really little kid again. If I was going to visit a relative, she'd call them up ahead of time and make sure they were going to cook only food I could eat, no matter who else they had to cook for. I didn't know what to do. I didn't want to hurt my mother's feelings but even my relatives were getting tired of having me around because they had to treat me like I would break if they did one thing wrong. Finally, one day I was supposed to go on a trip with my school to see a play and have dinner out. Mom said she was going to call the teacher to give her instructions on how to watch what I ordered. I knew I had to do something. As gently as I could, I asked her not to call the teacher. I told her I was a teenager and knew what to eat and what not to eat. She didn't have to worry that I was going to order a plate of french fries and a big chocolate shake. I told her how I felt about her telling everyone. At first her feelings were hurt but I let her know that I knew she thought she'd been doing right by me. She finally agreed not to call the teacher if I could show her for the time left before the trip that I was responsible enough to care for myself."

105

Some parents, like Tanisha's mother, feel a need to prepare everyone to monitor their child's diabetes. If your parents are like this, it may be up to you to make the first move and let them know how you feel about their telling people. You may have to demonstrate to them that you can behave responsibly and watch your diet carefully before they let you do so.

Pessimistic Parents

Sometimes parents react to learning a child has diabetes with pessimism. If you hear your parents saying things like "Oh, John will never live a normal life" or "Poor Mary, she'll never grow up to have any children," your first reaction might be to believe them. DON'T. You know that with proper care you can control your diabetes and live a relatively normal life AND have children. If your parents express negative thoughts about your illness, talk to them. Tell them that what they say makes you feel bad. They are probably not aware that what they are saying is having any effect on you. They aren't saying things to be mean, but rather because they love you and are frightened. If necessary, ask your health care provider to talk to them and give them more information. The key to understanding and coping with anything is knowledge. The more you know about something, the easier it is for you to deal with it, diabetes included.

Brothers and Sisters

Brothers and sisters will probably experience the same feelings that you and your parents do but with some other feelings as well. While they may accept the initial extra attention that your diagnosis focuses on you, after a while they may begin to resent it. They may feel that your mother or father is neglecting them—that somehow you have become more special and more important to everyone than they are. They may act out and say mean, hateful things to you as a way of expressing their resentment. They may accuse you of deliberately getting sick in order to get all the attention.

Although it may feel good to be the center of attention for a while, this can cause other problems in the family. You will always have diabetes but you will not always be a child or a teenager. If you and other family members belong to a diabetes support group, this is an issue that could be addressed during a support meeting. Maybe other members could help your parents understand that too much attention is not good for the rest of the family. And too much attention is not good for you either. You need to be developing the skills and the responsibilities you will need as an adult. After all you don't really want your parents to take care of you forever, do you?

Sometimes, having diabetes means that you have to grow up and accept more responsibility sooner than you or your family had planned. You may be the one who sometimes has to take the initiative for things. If your siblings are acting out because you have diabetes, try and talk to your parents about your concerns for your sisters and brothers. Be honest about how you feel. Ask them to help you talk with your brother or sister. If they are not responsive, then you can make it easier by showing your brother or sister more attention yourself. Try to understand that they don't mean the careless things they say.

The Pinatelli Family's Story

When Eddie Pinatelli was diagnosed with diabetes, he was fifteen years old and his brother, Vinnie, was eight. Vinnie had been the "baby" in the family as long as he could remember but when Eddie came home from the hospital after his diagnosis, all of that changed. When Eddie came home, many relatives came over to welcome him home and show their concern. No one seemed to notice Vinnie. He just stood at the back of the room and hoped that someone would notice him, but no one did. Everyone was focused on Eddie and how he was doing. Vinnie waited for things to return to "normal," but they didn't. During the following weeks, Mrs. Pinatelli spent almost all day caring for her older son and most of the evening still tending to Eddie plus caring for her husband. Mr. Pinatelli was still the same, but he worked all day and was too tired to play with Vinnie. It wasn't long before Vinnie started to feel left out. He couldn't see any visible change in Eddie. He still looked the same to Vinnie. All he knew was that his mother and the other relatives had been giving Eddie a lot more attention than they had before. There were special snacks in the kitchen that were just for Eddie. When Vinnie would take one, his mom would get mad. Meals were planned around what Eddie could eat and when he could eat it. It seemed that whatever Eddie wanted, his mom would do. If the family decided to go to the movies, Eddie got to pick the movie. If a family outing was planned and Eddie said he didn't feel well, the outing was canceled. Eddie got to stay *home from school a lot while Vinnie had to go even when he didn't feel so great. Vinnie started to resent Eddie and one day just exploded. Vinnie was watching his favorite cartoon on television when Eddie came into the family room and switched the channel without even asking. Vinnie started shouting. "I hate you. I hate you. Ever since you got sick, everybody does anything you want. I wish you would hurry up and die."*

How do you think Eddie felt when he heard his brother say this?

How would you feel if you were Eddie?

Would you have done anything differently if you had been Eddie?

How did Vinnie feel?

Could this have been avoided? How or why not?

When a child, no matter how old, is diagnosed with a disease, it is natural for other family members to rally around that child to give comfort and aid. But it is important to remember that other members of the family continue to need attention, affection, and comfort as well. While a sick person may require a lot of care, it doesn't mean that others, especially young children, will understand.

When someone is diagnosed with diabetes, it's time for the family to begin to develop a support network. Other family members, teachers, and health care professionals can and should work together to provide support not only for the person with diabetes but for all members of the family. The Pinatellis could have had help from a variety of sources. The relatives could have been cautioned to pay attention to Vinnie as well as Eddie. And although Mrs. Pinatelli assumed responsibility for monitoring and caring for Eddie, the family should have allowed Eddie to begin to assume responsibility for caring for himself. If Eddie was not feeling well enough to go to a family outing, other plans could have been made to do something fun at home or either Mr. or Mrs. Pinatelli could have taken Vinnie out. In addition having diabetes is no reason for you to pick the movie or television show. The fact that Eddie has diabetes has an effect on the family but should not determine everything about how the family functions. Also, someone should have taken the time to talk with Vinnie about the disease and what it meant. He also should have been reassured that Eddie was not going to die.

After his outburst, the Pinatellis recognized that Vinnie was feeling left out. They took more time to include him and even asked him to help Eddie with his finger sticks. They made sure that there were snacks for Vinnie as well as Eddie. Mr. Pinatelli became more involved. And very important, they allowed Eddie to begin to take responsibility for the control of his disease so that diabetes no longer controlled the family, but Eddie controlled the diabetes.

Younger brothers and sisters may worry that diabetes is contagious and may stay away from you. Explain to them that diabetes is not caused by germs so they cannot get it by being close to you. Encourage them to help you in your daily care. Let them watch you do a finger stick or give yourself insulin. This may take some of the fear away from them. If they are old enough, you might even let them do the finger stick for you.

Sometimes brothers or sisters may fear getting the disease not because it's contagious but because they know that heredity plays a part in determining who gets diabetes. Brothers and sisters of someone with diabetes have a 10 percent chance of getting the disease.

Bernadette's Story

"I learned I had diabetes three years ago when I was eleven. My sister, Maryann, was nine then. My mom told her all about diabetes and how it wasn't contagious and that she didn't need to worry about getting it. Maryann seemed to accept my diabetes and never asked any more questions. Last year, she started asking a lot of questions. She wanted to help me do my monitoring and give me my shots, so I let her. One day I came home from school early, and I found Maryann in my room sticking her finger. She had all my monitoring equipment out. I started yelling at her, and my mom came in to see what was going on. She took Maryann out of the room. Later Mom told me that some kid at school had told Maryann that because we were sisters, she was going to get diabetes some day too. She had been monitoring her blood sugar all week. Mom said she was going to make an appointment with the pediatrician to have Maryann get an islet-cell antibody test. She explained that an islet-cell antibody test could tell years in advance if someone was going to get Type I diabetes."

Your brothers and sisters may worry that you are going to die soon. Reassure them that you are going to be fine. Young children do not understand the concept of death or even of disease. Again give them information. Tell them how the availability of insulin has allowed people with diabetes to live very long lives. Show them that you take care of yourself so that they can understand that you are not going to die soon. Tell them stories of other people with diabetes who are leading productive and full lives. If your parents don't explain to them about diabetes, you can relieve some of their fears by giving them as much information as you can. Do not underestimate their ability to understand.

You may feel that it is not your job to reassure your brothers and sisters or to be the strong one in your family. While it is not your job alone, as a member of the family you do have an obligation to take your turn. Not everyone can be strong all the time. That's why families are so important. If you are feeling resentful, you need to talk to other family members and let them know how you feel. At the same time you need to be aware that they may have their own fears, concerns, and resentments. You and your family may have to learn to communicate more effectively not only for the well-being of the family but for your own well-being. Chronic stress can aggravate diabetes. Family support is one of the most important tools anyone can have. That doesn't mean that your parents should do everything for you. Nor does it mean you should do everything for yourself. Family support means working together, trying to understand the balance between doing too much and doing too little. It means listening to and understanding what others are saying as well.

Diabetes and Your School
Coping with Teachers and School Administrators

Although you do not have to tell anyone at your school that you have diabetes, it is best to let someone know. No matter what age you are when you are diagnosed with diabetes, it is advisable for you and your parents to meet with the proper school authorities to discuss your diabetes. You will probably want to meet with the school nurse and your particular teachers.

Your teachers and the school nurse need to receive as much information as possible about diabetes and about your experience with diabetes. Don't presume that anyone already knows all about diabetes. There may be some basic misconceptions and fears that you and your parents can correct by providing current information. If you have special needs, then your teachers need to know about them. You may carry food such as orange juice or cheese and crackers in case of an insulin reaction. You may need to have a snack in the middle of a class when there is a rule that no eating is allowed. You have a right to expect the school to be flexible with its rules in order to accommodate your special needs. You may have to get written permission from your doctor to perform finger sticks and take insulin while you are at school.

Different schools may have different rules. Some schools may allow you to perform finger sticks in the classroom while others may require that you go to the nurse's office or the bathroom. Also, unless your parents request it, you do not need a nurse to be present while you perform a finger stick or inject insulin. No matter where you do finger sticks or inject insulin, be sure to carry some sort of container to put the lancets and syringes in so that you can dispose of them properly. Diabetes is not contagious but someone could get a serious infection if he or she accidentally got stuck with a used lancet or syringe. Be considerate of others.

Make certain the proper school officials are aware that you inject insulin and need to use a syringe. With today's high incidence of substance abuse in schools you do not want to be wrongly accused of using drugs. Even though everyone would eventually realize a mistake had been made, you would have been subjected to an unnecessary stressful situation. Try to get all of this information straight before there is a problem at school.

Your diabetes may require that you have more absences than the attendance policy allows. Your school does not have the right to punish you for this by failing you in subjects where your grades were good or by not allowing you to make up the work you missed. Try to avoid attendance policy problems by discussing this with your teachers and school administrators at the beginning of each school year. You must also do your part by keeping your grades up and keeping up with schoolwork even while you are at home, if you can.

Your school does not have the right to single you out or prevent you from going on field trips or participating in athletic activities because you have diabetes.

Having diabetes does not mean you cannot take trips with your class. If you are being singled out as someone who cannot go because of your diabetes, you have a right to complain. Diabetes does not hinder travel. If your class is planning on eating out, you know what you should and should not eat. You will be taking your insulin or medication with you just as you always do so that you are prepared for the ordinary events and even extraordinary events, such as hypoglycemia.

Ruth's Story

Ruth was diagnosed with diabetes when she was three years old. Over the years she learned to take control of her diabetes, and her parents encouraged her to become a responsible partner in her own care and let her go on an insulin pump. She always participated in all school activities and made straight A's even though she sometimes had to take a sick day off. When Ruth was thirteen, her mother got a new job in a different city and the family had to move. Ruth was sad about leaving her old school but excited about making new friends. She didn't think about explaining her diabetes to anyone because she had been living with it for almost ten years and it was just a way of life to her. Her parents filled out all the medical forms at school and included the fact that Ruth had diabetes. Ruth arrived at her new school just in time for a class trip to the circus. Her mother signed her permission slip to go but when the day for the trip came, Ruth was made to stay in the library. When Ruth's mother found out about it, she called the school and demanded to know what had happened. The teacher explained that because Ruth had diabetes and there were so many opportunities to eat "bad" food at the circus, the teacher and the school nurse decided that it would be unsafe for Ruth to go because it would be too tempting.

Once again, you can see the result of people not knowing the facts about diabetes. You also see the problems that can occur when someone assumes that because you have diabetes you will act in a certain way. The American Diabetes Association continues to emphasize that each person with diabetes ought to be considered as an individual not just as a person with diabetes. Ruth had been managing her diabetes for some time. There was no reason to assume that she would eat "bad" food at the circus and risk raising her blood sugar levels. Ruth's mother immediately found a local support group for people with diabetes and arranged for a diabetes educator to speak with the teacher and the nurse.

School sports is another area where you might have to assert yourself. If you want to participate in athletic activities and your diabetes in under control, there is no reason why you shouldn't. Unfortunately, some school personnel are not fully informed about diabetes.

Carlos's Story

Carlos had been playing baseball since he was in Little League. When he was in junior high school, he was captain of the team. The coach at this new high school recruited Carlos for the team, and he played second base during ninth grade and was supposed to play the same position when baseball season came around the next year. During the third month of tenth grade, Carlos was out of school for a week. At first his parents thought it was just the flu, but when Carlos didn't seem to get better, they took him to the doctor. The doctor did some tests and diagnosed Carlos with Type I diabetes. Carlos and his parents met with Carlos's health care team and worked together to help him control his diabetes. With the help of his health care team and family he was able to keep his diabetes under control. He learned to do his SMBGs before and after exercise. He knew to eat a carbohydrate snack just before practice. He could recognize the signs of low blood sugar and knew when to slow down. By the time baseball season came around, Carlos was ready. The first day of practice, Carlos showed up on the field. The coach told him that he wasn't on the team this year because of his diabetes. Carlos tried to explain that he had his diabetes under control but the coach wouldn't listen.

What happened to Carlos is not uncommon. Many people do not really understand diabetes and how it works. But Carlos did not have to accept what happened. The coach was discriminating against Carlos simply because he was a diabetic. Carlos could have been more assertive when he talked to the coach. He could have told the coach that people with Type I diabetes participate in all forms of sports. Carlos could have asked a diabetes educator or his doctor to talk to the coach. And, as a last resort, Carlos could have gone to the school administration to plead his case.

Every day does not have to be a fight for your rights, but if something is really important to you, such as playing baseball was to Carlos, then you have to stand up for yourself. It is not always easy to be assertive, but, with practice, it becomes easier.

If you are involved in athletics, make certain your coach or physical education teacher can recognize the difference between hypoglycemia (low blood sugar) and hyperglycemia (high blood sugar). If your coach or physical education teacher doesn't know very much about diabetes, take some time to share the information you have. Teach him or her how to give and read a glucose test. This is important for him or her to know anyway. Sometimes the best approach is to educate rather than wait until an incident occurs.

You have a right to be accepted by teachers and peers. In return, the school and your teachers have a right to expect you to be honest about your condition, to provide them with the information necessary to help them care for you in the event of an emergency.

If people in your school are not respectful of your rights, they may be guilty of discrimination. Your school does not have a right to require that you take your insulin only before or after class. If you can do it at those times, that is terrific, but if you can't, you have a right to inject your insulin whenever you are supposed to do it. Your school does not have the right to prevent you from eating a necessary snack. Your school does not have the right to prevent you from making up work missed because of sick days.

Occasionally schools have problems with diabetic students who use the disease as an excuse to cut class. If your school has had this problem, you may find that the teacher is unwilling to work with you to help you manage your diabetes. If that is the case, there are several things you can try. First, remind the teacher that you are not that student and that each student should be judged on a case by case basis. Remind your teacher that diabetics are individuals just like any other group. People with diabetes share a disease not personalities or habits. If your teacher is not persuaded, ask someone on your health care team to call your school. If this is unsuccessful, there are legal options.

Schools have something called the "504" plan which allows students to request "accommodations" due to missed days. This means that your school is required to allow you to make up work missed without penalty. The 504 plan protects students who are considered to have "a disability in one of life's functions." The wide fluctuation in blood sugar is an impairment in a life function. Also, your school has a "Health Impaired" section under its special education rules that allows you to make up missed work.

Coping with Classmates

If your classmates are aware that you have diabetes, they may ask you questions about it. Some of the questions will be about taking insulin. Questions such as: "Does it hurt?" "How can you stand taking those shots every day?" "Aren't you afraid that you'll stick yourself in the wrong place?" Some of these questions are the very same ones you asked when you first learned you had diabetes. The best approach to these questions is to answer truthfully. Usually that is the end of it. It is possible that you will have a classmate who is not very sensitive and who keeps asking you questions that become annoying. Or you may have a classmate who doesn't really know that much about diabetes and repeats many of the myths in order to hurt your feelings or make you angry.

Elliot's Story

Elliot was diagnosed with diabetes when he was twelve years old. He never had any trouble with any of his classmates until he entered high school. Elliot had gone to middle school with the same kids that lived in his neighborhood. But the high school was the only school for many neighborhoods, so there were plenty of new faces in his classes that year. Elliot's parents made sure that his teachers, the school administration, and the school nurse knew that he was required to take insulin shots during times when he would be in class. They had agreed that it would not be a problem as far as they were concerned. One day during English class, another student stared at Elliot while he was doing a finger stick and giving himself an injection. He didn't say anything to Elliot until after class. Then he asked Elliot if he was a "sugar baby." Elliot tried to explain that he had diabetes, but the boy just called him "sugar baby" again and went off laughing. The next day at school there was a note taped to Elliot's locker. On the front the note said "To the Sugar Baby." Inside was a picture of an overweight boy eating a candy bar. Elliot knew who had left the note but he didn't tell anyone about it. It was hard for him to concentrate on his schoolwork, and when he went home, he was still so upset that he couldn't eat dinner.

How would you handle this situation if you were Elliot? Would you confront the other student? Would you tell the teacher?

Probably the first thing Elliot should have done was talk to one of his friends. Friends are there to listen to us. Elliot's feelings were hurt and he kept that to himself. If you have problems that you can't solve or don't know how to deal with, talking to your friends may be helpful. They may be able to offer solutions or help by just listening and taking your side. It is important to have a support network of teachers, friends, and family. It is also important to use that network in times of stress. Having your feelings hurt by an insensitive classmate creates stress. And stress can alter glucose levels.

Another thing Elliot could have done was to stand up for himself the first time the other student called him names. That isn't always easy. Being assertive can be very difficult or frightening. But if you know you are being treated unfairly or if hurtful things are being said about you, stand up for yourself. Explain yourself to the person. This may or may not help the person understand your situation, but the important thing is that you have asserted yourself. When you do that you increase your own self-esteem. You know that you did everything you could to solve the problem.

Sometimes being assertive doesn't work. If that's the case, you may have to go to others for help. Perhaps Elliot could have spoken with the teacher and suggested a way he could inform the class about his diabetes. Because it was English class, maybe the teacher could have assigned an essay on sensitivity or even on diabetes. It may seem unfair that Elliot should be the one to find a solution, but that's part of growing up and becoming a responsible adult. Or Elliot could have just told the teacher and let him or her handle the problem. Remember, you are not alone. You have friends and family to comfort you, and you have teachers and other people at the school to intervene for you if you need them to. But most of all, you have yourself, and you are learning just how strong you are each and every day.

Diabetes and the Future

Because diabetes is a chronic disease that so far has no known cure, the way diabetes affects your future depends very much on what you do to take care of yourself today. But there is some general information that you as a diabetic need to know about the world we live in. Although diabetes cannot be cured, it can be controlled and because of this there are very few limitations for you. Federal law does prohibit people with insulin-dependent diabetes from serving in the armed forces, holding jobs as pilots, or holding jobs that require driving interstate vehicles. States or cities may have similar restrictions but for the most part employers are urged to take each individual as an individual. These laws are being challenged by many people as a result of the Americans with Disabilities Act (ADA) of 1992. Since then more than 1,000 cases of job discrimination have been filed by people with diabetes. A few years ago, Ken Drugger, who has Type I diabetes, successfully sued the Bureau of Alcohol, Tobacco and Firearms, forcing it to reconsider its policy of not allowing people with insulin-dependent diabetes to become criminal investigators or special agents. It took Mr. Drugger seven years to obtain his victory, but it is a victory for everyone with diabetes. Also the ADA is working to revoke the ban against allowing people with diabetes to obtain commercial driver's licenses and pilot's licenses. You are not required to tell an employer that you have diabetes.

Marriage and Children

Diabetes should not prevent you from getting married and having children. If you are a woman with diabetes, you will need to practice tight control in order to maintain acceptable blood sugar levels when you are pregnant. You will probably see your doctor more than a pregnant woman without diabetes would. However, having diabetes should never stand in the way of leading a full and productive life.

Current Research

Technology
Researchers are working on several types of noninvasive glucose monitors. One device under study uses near-infrared light that passes through the finger and "takes a picture" of what it sees, including the glucose in the blood.

Another type of monitor being worked on is a skin patch that could extract glucose through the skin.

Research is also being done on an implanted monitor that would monitor glucose levels all day long.

Insulin delivery
Researchers seem to be near a solution to oral insulin.

They have developed a small "bead" of protective material that would surround the insulin and prevent a person's digestive juices from destroying it. This would eliminate the need for injections for many people.

Transplants

Scientists at the University of Massachusetts are working on a method to transplant islet-cells from a healthy pancreas to a person with diabetes. Canadian researchers are working on the same type of program. These transplants are important because they would enable the body of a person with diabetes to produce normal levels of insulin on its own.

The NIDDKD is doing a study to see if insulin therapy before the onset of Type I diabetes can prevent it in those who test positive in tests like the islet-cell antibody test.

Be Prepared

All the things you need to do to control your diabetes may seem pretty overwhelming, especially if you have just been diagnosed. It is true that diabetes can affect every aspect of your life, but diabetes does not have to control your life if you are willing to control your diabetes. Sometimes it is hard enough just being a teenager without having the complications of diabetes. Remember, you did nothing to get diabetes. It is not caused by eating candy bars. Scientists do not yet know why some people get diabetes and others don't. Having diabetes means that you need to control your balance of insulin and glucose in order to prevent hypoglycemia (low blood sugar) and hyperglycemia (high blood sugar) and to avoid or delay future complications. You do this through diet, exercise, and sometimes medication or insulin depending on the type of diabetes you have. Just because you don't take insulin doesn't mean your diabetes isn't serious. All diabetes is serious and potentially life-threatening. There are some basic things to do if you have diabetes:

➭ Monitor your glucose levels regularly and keep an accurate log of those readings

➭ Get into a routine of checking your body for scratches or cuts or sores

126

↪ Practice good oral and body hygiene

↪ Eat a healthy diet with plenty of fruits, vegetables, and fiber

↪ Read the labels on food to find out the ingredients

↪ Exercise regularly

↪ If you take insulin, make certain you follow your doctor's instructions and be sure you are always prepared with an emergency insulin kit

↪ See your dentist regularly

↪ Have yearly eye exams

↪ Get a flu shot each fall

↪ If you get sick, call your doctor

↪ Give yourself a pat on the back now and then for a job well done

There are also some basic things not to do if you have diabetes:

↪ Don't smoke

↪ Don't use alcohol and recreational drugs

↪ Don't wear tight clothing, especially on your legs and feet

↪ Don't stop taking insulin or any other medication unless your doctor tells you to stop

➥ Don't try to fix ingrown toenails yourself

Follow these tips to better prepare for handling diabetes:

➥ Always keep extra supplies of insulin or oral medications handy for emergencies. Know the type of
   medication or insulin you take and how much.

➥ Have your doctor's phone number with you all the
   time. Know how to reach him or her on the weekends, at night, or on holidays.

➥ Have a plan for sick days before you get sick.
   Follow the sick day guidelines and the advice of
   your doctor.

➥ Because fluctuating levels of glucose are the most
   common cause of complications for people with
   diabetes, it is a good idea to review how to manage
   them.

➥ Frequent testing will usually let you know if your
   glucose levels need to be treated with insulin, exercise, or food. Keeping good records will help you
   see if there is a pattern to your glucose levels so
   that you can anticipate complications before they
   occur.

➥ You need to make the people around you aware of
   the differences between hypoglycemia and hyperglycemia and what to do to treat either one of
   them.

☞ It is important to understand that the better you control your diabetes, the less chance you have of developing complications related to diabetes.

Remember, you are not alone. You have your health care team for your medical needs. You have friends and family for your emotional needs. And there are millions of people with diabetes throughout the world. Some of them live in your own neighborhood. Meet them and share your experiences and learn from theirs. Don't let diabetes control your life. Make it your job to control your diabetes. Good luck!

Appendix

MYTHS AND FACTS ABOUT DIABETES

Myth: Diabetes is caused by eating too many sweet things.
Fact: Diabetes is caused by a lack of insulin, NOT an excess of sweets. When people talk about "blood sugar," they are referring to glucose, not candy bars. Our bodies get glucose for energy by breaking down carbohydrates, fats, and proteins. Carbohydrates are the biggest source of glucose because 100 percent of a carbohydrate turns into glucose. By comparison, 60 percent of proteins and 10 percent of fats are broken down into glucose. When glucose enters the bloodstream, the body releases insulin to help carry the glucose to cells throughout the body. It is normal for the blood to have a certain level of glucose for future energy needs. When a person does not have enough insulin in the bloodstream, however, the glucose builds up to such a level that it "spills" over into the urine.

Myth: Having diabetes means that you can never have any extra snacks or sweets.
Fact: If you are controlling your diabetes, you can have extra snacks and sweets, but like everything else, this must be done in moderation. You can even eat at fast-food restaurants if you are careful about what you select.

Remember, a diet for people with diabetes is the same healthy diet that is good for everyone.

Myth: Diabetes is contagious.
Fact: Diabetes is NOT contagious. You cannot "catch" diabetes the way people "catch" colds. Just because you or someone else in your family has diabetes doesn't mean others will get it too. A person who has family members with diabetes is more likely to get diabetes than a person who comes from a family with no history of diabetes because of heredity, not closeness.

Myth: When you get diabetes, your life is over.
Fact: Hearing a diagnosis of diabetes may seem like the end of the world but it isn't. You can take control of your diabetes and live a very full life. It's a decision only you can make. Having diabetes does make you grow up a lot faster in some ways. In order to control your diabetes, you must take responsibility for yourself to a greater degree than most teenagers without diabetes do.

Myth: People with diabetes will die younger than people without diabetes.
Fact: If a person was diagnosed with diabetes before the 1920s, he or she could expect to be dead within the year. Since the discovery and utilization of insulin, people with diabetes can live as long as people without diabetes.

Myth: Having diabetes means you can never have children.
Fact: People with diabetes are having children every day. Women with diabetes who become pregnant can, with

proper care and control of their diabetes, have healthy babies just like everyone else.

Myth: Hair permanents will not stay in people with diabetes.
Fact: Diabetes and hair permanents have no effect on each other. A person with diabetes can use makeup, hair coloring, and permanents just like everyone else.

Myth: People with diabetes cannot wear artificial finger nails.
Fact: Diabetes has no effect on artificial nails. If you have diabetes, you certainly can wear artificial nails if you want to, especially if you make certain to keep your hands and nails clean. The only precaution, however, is that if you are going to use artificial nails, be careful. This is a precaution everyone who wears artificial nails should follow. If you wear artificial nails for too long without taking them off, you may develop a fungal infection underneath the nails. If you wear artificial nails, watch for this. At the first sign, stop wearing them!

Myth: People with diabetes cannot have their ears pierced.
Fact: While it is true that many establishments ask customers to sign a waiver that they do not have diabetes before they can get their ears pierced, there really isn't a good reason for this policy. Although people with diabetes may get infections more easily than people without diabetes, if a person's blood sugar levels are good and the person is in reasonable health, there is no reason not to go ahead with ear piercing.

Myth: Urine tests are obsolete.
Fact: While urine tests are no longer used for measuring blood sugar because of their inaccuracies, they are still necessary for measuring ketones, which blood sugar tests don't measure.

Myth: Having the doctor check your glucose level once every couple of months is just as good as using home testing every day.
Fact: Research has shown that "tight control" is the best way to prevent or delay diabetes complications. The only way to achieve "tight" control is through frequent daily testing.

Myth: Diabetes develops suddenly.
Fact: Diabetes develops over several years. Because the symptoms of diabetes appear suddenly, some people think that diabetes occurs "just like that." In fact, there is a test called the islet-cell antibody test that can tell if someone will develop diabetes in the future. The test works because the antibodies acting to protect the body appear long before the disease itself does.

Myth: The insulin pump is practically a cure for diabetes.
Fact: The insulin pump is an insulin delivery system and NOT an artificial pancreas. The insulin pump allows its user a lot more freedom because there are fewer injections, but the insulin pump requires even more work from its user than other insulin delivery systems. There is no cure for diabetes right now.

Myth: Drinking aloe juice is a good way to control diabetes. **Fact:** Aloe juice is not a substitute for insulin, and it does not help control diabetes. There are many "alternative" therapies for diabetes on the market. Drinking aloe juice is just one of them. When a person has a chronic disease like diabetes, it can be easy to become attracted to advertisers who claim new cures. While the aloe juice cure does no physical harm, except to the buyer's purse, there are other alternative therapies that can be very dangerous. Always consult with your health care team about the claims made for alternative therapies. Chromium is another alternative therapy that has been said to cure diabetes. While chromium deficiencies have been known to increase blood sugar and glucose intolerance, they do not cause diabetes. Diabetes is a result of inadequate or no insulin, not a lack of chromium. Never abandon your traditional therapy of balancing insulin, exercise, and diet for unsubstantiated alternative therapies.

Myth: Type II diabetes is not as serious as Type I diabetes. **Fact:** Type II diabetes is every bit as serious as Type I. Diabetes complications usually take longer to develop in people with Type II diabetes, but they will develop, especially if the person hasn't taken control of the disease. If you have Type II diabetes, don't ever think that just because you don't take insulin, you don't have to take good care of yourself! The complications for people with Type I diabetes are eye, kidney, and nerve damage. The complications for people with Type II diabetes are heart disease, stroke, high blood pressure, and foot problems. You can see that the complications are serious no matter which type of diabetes you have.

Myth: People with Type II diabetes don't have to take insulin.
Fact: At least 25 percent and up to 50 percent of Type IIs will be required to take insulin during their lifetimes. Although in Type II diabetes there is too much insulin in the bloodstream, eventually the pancreas may begin to shut down. That means that there is no longer enough insulin in the bloodstream. That's why it is very important for people with Type II diabetes to get their weight under control and to exercise regularly. Those are the two main keys to controlling Type II diabetes and to delaying or preventing the use of insulin and future complications.

Myth: Only people who are overweight get diabetes.
Fact: Although being overweight has been associated with Type II diabetes, you don't have to be overweight to get it. Most young people who are diagnosed with diabetes are not overweight.

Myth: A cure for diabetes is just around the corner, so it's okay not to take good care of yourself right now.
Fact: Maybe there is a cure just around the corner, but maybe there isn't. Researchers and scientists are working hard every day to learn more about diabetes and its complications. But it seems the more they learn, the more they see there is to learn. To lessen the chance of severe complications from diabetes as you get older, diabetes must always be kept under control

Glossary

basal dose The lowest dose of insulin that can be continually injected.

blood sugar Also known as blood glucose, it's the amount of sugar found in the bloodstream.

bolus dose A large dose of insulin taken before meals or snacks.

dawn phenomenon A high blood sugar count (hyperglycemia) upon waking up in the morning.

diabetes mellitus Medical term for diabetes.

DKA (Diabetic Ketoacidosis) A high amount of glucose in the blood that can lead to a diabetic coma.

endocrinologist A doctor who specializes in the glands of the body that manufacture hormones.

endorphins Hormones released by the body that makes a person feel good.

finger stick Method of obtaining a drop of blood to test for glucose.

glaucoma Eye disease marked by increasing pressure within the eyeball that can result in loss of vision.

glucose A simple sugar that the body converts from food to provide energy to the body.

hyperglycemia Too much sugar in the bloodstream.

hypoglycemia Low amount of sugar in the bloodstream.

insulin Hormone produced by the pancreas that helps move glucose from the bloodstream into the cells where it can be used for energy.

insulin resistance Ineffective use of insulin by the body.

ketones The waste product of the body's breaking down fats to use for energy.

podiatrist A doctor who specializes in caring for the feet.

retinologist A doctor who specializes in caring for the eyes, especially the retina.

SMBG (self-monitoring of blood glucose) Daily testing of the glucose levels in the blood, often through the use of a finger stick and a blood glucose monitor.

Where to Go for Help

The American Dietetics Association/National Center for Nutrition and Dietetics
Consumer Nutrition Hotline (800) 366-1655.

American Association of Diabetes Educators
444 North Michigan Avenue
Suite 1240
Chicago, IL 60611-3901
(312) 644-2233
(800) 338-3633
(800) TEAMUP (for referral to a diabetes educator in your area)

American Dietetic Association
216 West Jackson Boulevard
Chicago, IL 60606
(800) 877-1600 ext. 4853

American Diabetes Association
Diabetes Information Service Center
1660 Duke Street
Alexandria, VA 22314
(800) 232-3472

International Diabetes Athletes Association
1647-B West Bethany Home Road
Phoenix, AZ 85015
(800) 898-IDAA

Juvenile Diabetes Foundation
120 Wall Street
New York, NY 1005-4001
(800) JDF-CURE

National Diabetes Information Clearinghouse
National Institute of Diabetes and Digestive and Kidney
    Diseases (NIDDKD)
1 Information Way
Bethesda, MD 20892-3560

The Weight Control Information Network
NIDDKD
1 Win Way
Bethesda, MD 20892
(800) WIN 8098

Web Sites

http://www.castleweb.com/diabetes/
http://www.cdc.gov/nccdphp/ddt/ddthome.htm
http://www.diabetes.com
http://www.diabetesnet.com
http://www.diabetes.org/
http://www.jdfcure.com
http://www.LifeScan.com

For Further Reading

Alvin, Virginia, and Robert Silverstein. *Diabetes.*Springfield, NJ: Enslow Publishers, 1994.

Betschart, Jean, and Susan Thom. *In Control—A Guide for Teens with Diabetes.* Minneapolis, MN: Chronimed, 1995.

Ferber, Elizabeth. *Diabetes: One Day at a Time.* Brookfield, CT: Millbrook Press, 1996

Landau, Elaine. *Understanding Illness: Diabetes.* New York: Twenty-First Century Books, 1994.

Little, Marjorie. *Diabetes.* New York: Chelsea House Publishing, 1991.

McManus, James. *Going to the Sun.* New York: HarperCollins, 1996.

Roberts, Willo Davis. *Sugar Isn't Everything.* New York: Atheneum, 1987.

Titles available through the American Diabetes Association
American Diabetes Association Complete Guide to Diabetes Care
Diabetes A to Z: What You Need to Know About Diabetes Simply Put
101 Tips for Staying Healthy and Avoiding Complications

Index

U

United States, 1, 15, 17, 21,
    22, 42, 73
University of Massachusetts,
    125
urination
  excessive (polyuria), 4, 8, 10,
    34, 37

W

weight
  loss, 5, 6, 10, 47, 50
  role it plays in diabetes, 5,
    22, 135
Weight Watchers, 50